Recent Titles by Frances Paige from Severn House

BLOOD TIES
THE CONFETTI BED
SO LONG AT THE FAIR
THE SWIMMING POOL

'Yet neither pleasure's art can joy my spirits,
Nor yet the other's distance comfort me,
Then it is thus: the passions of the mind,
That have their first conception by misdread,
Have after-nourishment and life by care;
And what was first but fear what might be done,
Grows elder now and cares it be not done.'

Pericles
William Shakespeare

PASSIONS OF THE MIND

PASSIONS
OF THE MIND

Frances Paige

This title first published in Great Britain 1999 by
SEVERN HOUSE PUBLISHERS LTD of
9–15 High Street, Sutton, Surrey SM1 1DF.
Originally published in 1974 in Great Britain under
the title *The Glass Wall* and pseudonym *Jane Wallace*.
This title first published in the U.S.A. 1999 by
SEVERN HOUSE PUBLISHERS INC of
595 Madison Avenue, New York, N.Y. 10022.

British Library Cataloguing in Publication Data

Paige, Frances
    Passions of the mind
    1. Love stories
    I. Title
    823.9'14 [F]

    ISBN 0-7278-5444-5

All situations in this publication are fictitious and
any resemblance to living persons is purely coincidental.

Printed and bound in Great Britain by
MPG Books Ltd, Bodmin, Cornwall.

I

That morning when Julia awoke, she turned over on her side, pulling up her knees to her stomach and curving her body as if to shield herself. Pity to get up, even for an important day, here in bed she was warmly protected as if in a womb. Warm red-black darkness. Could one really remember it, the suspended softness?

'Happy birthday,' they would all sing. 'Twenty-one today, twenty-one today . . . Never has had the key before . . .' But she had. For a long time. Progressive parents, but strangely old-fashioned in wishing to give her a formal dance

'Twenty-one today . . .' Hardly any young people at home when they were twenty-one, parents couldn't lay their hands on them, they were going the long way round to India, or hitching lifts on the N20 to Spain, or living it up in flats in London. The clever ones were working hard at a career and the sensible ones were married with children. Mother wanted her to be married. You knew that, catching her eye sometimes, the contemplation, the *wariness* . . . the wariness was the worrying part.

She isn't comfortable with me. I'm a disappointment . . . Insisting on leaving school early but being persuaded to go to Vevey to be 'finished', which was as old-fashioned as a twenty-first birthday dance. Then to please Father the abortive attempt at learning shorthand and typewriting with beauty culture thrown in as an unlikely extra (to please Mother), then to please both, the Cordon Bleu course in the Stately Home. Nothing

5

made any sense except the sculpting and sometimes that didn't make much sense either.

But nobody pushed you around too much at the Art School, and there was always the hope that it would give you the answer. The answer to what? She didn't know. All she knew was that the chaos which was unsolved in the clay meant something, must mean something, if she could only find the key.

'You've certainly got a problem there,' Danny had said, looking at her last effort. 'They say the reward is in the struggle. Well, rather you than me.' Danny was a part-time teacher at the Art School, a failed sculptor because of the booze. Hadn't he been able to find the answer either? But at least she was trying, not sitting in Harrods with Mother having a low calorie lunch, or clacking away at a typewriter all day, perhaps being beautifully made-up helped, or again, planning three course menus of stodge for kids or balanced diets for overweight tycoons.

She raised her head and noticed that the spoonback chair against the window cut out a dark curved segment at the bottom, leaving an interesting shape. And the shape was filled with the wych elm, weaving . . . a pity there was the May greenery, the snake-like branches were more rewarding in winter, but there were still traces of them breaking through the pale green which frothed round beige-coloured florets.

She looked, her eyes wide open. Why did some things hit her visually, assault her mind with their importance? Here the ingredients were simple, a spoonback chair, a wych elm and a window. But when you looked and looked again, the window frame became a picture frame, and within it there was an abstract pattern, shape upon shape, shape within shape. The branches were like some of Blake's drawings, contorted, wilful . . . my world at this moment has shrunk to consist only of this view through the window, contained in its rectangle, with the bite-

6

piece of the chair-back cutting off the left-hand corner. It's important, terribly important. Why is it important?

They'll both be coming in and they'll be saying 'Happy birthday, darling,' and Father will be jovial in his barrack-room style, 'Rise and shine!' Did they say that in the Army? And it wasn't true, was it, that they took the soldiers early morning tea? He was a joker.

She didn't want to rise and shine. She saw herself a curled-up shape lying on the bed, within a roomful of shapes, her tights a long limp double curve between the chair and the floor, the square bulge of the wardrobe, and round stool at the dressing-table, the horizontals of the skirting board running away from her, the perpendiculars of the flower-swathes on the wallpaper, busy, busy, busy . . .

A memory came from long ago when she had been digging in the wet sand with a little boy. It was Crawford, Crawford North, who often visited his grandparents in Dorset when she was visiting hers. The two houses lay near each other. 'Aren't they sweet together?' Grey heads nodding in deck chairs, huts on wheels. Beach weather. Sunny but with a cold wind which crept round corners, blew sand in your eyes.

A seagull had swooped suddenly above them and she had become that seagull, strong, beating wings, far below, mere specks on the sand, the wet shining sand, a little girl and a little boy. She could see the waves flattening themselves as they ran over the sand, lace-frilled. There was a red bucket, she swooped down on strong wings . . .

The door opened. It was Mother, Lydia, she wanted Julia to call her but it was too difficult, short hair brushed, trim housecoat tied at the front, loose back, she had lovely housecoats, when she bent to kiss Julia there was a clean, sweet smell, Lenthéric for mornings. 'Happy birthday, darling. A very special birthday. Aren't you going to get up to celebrate?'

And behind her was Father, handsome, spruce like Mother, she had never seen them in the in-between time, the frowsty time when they first rose, before they bathed. 'Rise and shine, Julia,' he was saying, 'rise and shine!' He bent over and kissed her, then tossed a pair of keys on a ring on the bed. 'For you,' he said, 'for your twenty-first. My God,' comically, clutching his forehead, 'we're a three car family now!'

'Thank you, thank you both.' She sat up and smiled. There should be proper words, loving words in which to thank this handsome pair. They stood waiting, smiling, and she said again, 'Oh, thank you! It's too much, I don't know what to say . . .' Her throat was suddenly rough with tears.

'Nothing's too much for the birthday girl.' Lydia's face was cool against hers, a beauty-treated face, slapped into fineness.

'Ta-ra-*boom*-de-day, this is my bi . . . rthday,' Father, Grant, he too would have liked his Christian name, sang out. 'Show a leg, then.' Mother kept on smiling, smiling.

It was better up. A kind of elation came in a whirl-wind of activity, breakfast with the detritus of the birth-day parcels spread about the table, helping her mother to direct the removal of the furniture from the billard room, the biggest room in the house. 'So useful for parties,' Lydia had said, cocktail parties, children's parties, she had a strongly developed social sense.

And then, a birthday treat, André arriving to dress their hair in a special birthday style. And not quite succeeding. It had ended by her mother having the same smooth cap, the hair swept round her ears and follow-ing the nape of her neck, and Julia's . . . 'Well, dear, it just seems to want to go its own sweet way, doesn't it?' But there had been a discreet difference, the subtle advertisement of André's skill.

The white dress, chosen by her mother, was too much of a ball dress. She had said so at the time but Lydia had worn her impatient look and said, 'Why must you always be so difficult?' And then to cover up had shrugged her shoulders at the saleswoman standing by and said, 'Girls . . .'

She would rather have had a zany kind of dress, the kind you wore lots of beads and chains with, and a band low down on her forehead like Hiawatha, but, having seen the look, she had said, 'It's lovely, it really is, Mother.' She thought, looking in the mirror, that it could have served as a wedding dress with the addition of a veil. Lydia's wishful thinking permeated it, the tiny waist, the sweeping folds. She wanted Julia to be a bride. To get married and leave home . . . no, that was unfair. This was her birthday and she was a beloved only child, in the garage there was proof of it, wasn't there, a white Triumph with red leather seats.

So here they were, in the shining-floored billiard room, an impressive tableau, ready to receive the guests. Lydia had wanted a marquee, but May weather could be treacherous and she had compromised with a tented ceiling and fairy lights.

The hall, which was lined with trestle tables loaded with food, had been inspected, the head waiter had been complimented. The food was as much a caterer's triumph as André's expertise had been. 'Will it do, Julia?'

'Do!' And then seeing the waiting smiles, 'It's superb!' It was, of course. Prawn cocktails, hors-d'œuvres, jellied consommé, chicken and curry, risotto, game pie, cold salmon, cold turkey, sweets of all kinds to be plundered, their careful decoration desecrated, and the cake, as virginally white as the dress.

The group had arrived in their fringed jackets and beads, and had been strangely polite and formal. She saw that underneath the gear they were ordinary lads from the Comprehensive. 'Yes, Mr. Fairfield, we'll keep it down a bit, yes, we get it, no Isle of Wight stuff.' The

9

leader had hair the same colour as Julia's and as silky. His décolletage showed a hairless chest. The drummer had a Cyrano de Bergerac nose.

Lydia's dress was deep turquoise to match the ring which Grant had given her on their twenty-fifth wedding anniversary. He had had his share of anniversaries lately, 'I've got two expensive women!' All her clothes were jewel-coloured, it made dressing easier, the proviso being that you had to have lots of jewels.

Grant was spruce but old-fashioned in his dinner jacket. His hair was too short and his cummerbund a disaster. 'Will I do?' he asked, so well-shaved, so full of bonhomie, so happy. 'Musn't let the side down.'

'Oh Father! I like your cummerbund . . .' And to Lydia, 'Your dress is beautiful, Mother, the exact shade . . .' You had to appease her.

The champagne which they had drunk to engender the festive spirit made her head feel light. I'm happy, she thought, she would have liked to dance to the soft drumming noise from the group. Father did a few awkward jigging steps beside her and she giggled behind her hand. Through the door she could see the waiters and waitresses standing behind the mountain of food which was criminal when you thought of Biafra, but you hadn't to think of things like that on your twenty-first. Mrs. Leighton and her minions were gossiping quietly in the kitchen, their paper carriers at the ready behind the door for the left-overs. Perhaps Balham was as needful as Biafra.

I'm happy . . . the group leader's face was soft and kind, small-chinned. He was of the new breed, bisexual, giving you, if you should need it, the best of both worlds, love and sympathy, empathy. But why should she need it? Why should she wish that somewhere in the world there was someone who would sit down and listen to her, who would open the door and take her in . . . perhaps that's what the Key of the Door was for. 'Never been twenty-one before . . .' She felt light, weightless, like a tethered balloon between Lydia and Grant, two stanchions. *I'm grateful, don't think I'm not grateful, I only wish I could show you how grateful I am . . .*

'Fate seems to throw us together,' Kate said, and, smilingly, 'I've nothing to do with it.' Lawrence had called for her because their flats were a stone's throw from each other in Old Brompton Road. Both came from Cheltenham, and both worked in the same publishers, Kate in foreign sales, Lawrence a newly appointed director. Certainly fate had been busy, she thought.

He had come heralded and much sung about from a rival firm. The girls in Fairfield and Wainwright had been all agog, had thought Kate had pulled a fast one because she discovered that they had known each other as children.

'Your rise in publishing has been meteoric,' she said, checking her handbag, 'not to mention that all our girls are swooning for love of you.'

He ignored that. 'You don't do so badly yourself. Rumour has it that you're a kingpin in your own department. With me it's luck, with you it's brains. That's why I jumped at the idea of escorting you tonight. I thought some of it might rub off.'

'Flattery will get you nowhere. Would you like a drink?'

'If we've time I'd love one.'

She said, 'Gin?' and when he nodded, 'Sweet or dry?'

'Just tonic if you've got it. Must leave plenty of room for the champagne. Oh, thanks.' She had put a glass and a bottle on a table beside him.

'You haven't seen the fair Julia, have you?'

'Actually, no. Is she a spoiled only?'

'I don't think she's that, extra sensitive, I'd say, other times she has a childlike gaiety. Sometimes you feel you want to touch her to see if she's real. I think, Lydia, her mother, can be a bit overpowering. Anyhow, form your own opinion. Julia will bowl you over sideways in any case. She's a natural beauty. Dresden. You can see the blue veins.'

'It would be difficult to outdo your charms.' Or yours, Kate thought, looking at him. He was handsome, a thin, clever face, charming smile, twenty-eight, (she had worked out his age), and even if he had been ordinary a directorship with Fairfield and Wainwright would have made him more than eligible. But he wasn't ordinary. He had the broad brow of a visionary. If he committed himself, he would commit himself wholly. Meantime he remained fancy free as far as she knew, and it was probably a feather in her cap that he had fallen in with Grant Fairfield's suggestion to escort her.

He was toasting her with upraised glass, looking around. 'Nice place you've got here. Do you live alone?'

'Yes. I made a crashing mistake which made me wary. I shacked up with a girl . . .' she laughed, 'a very nice chap.'

He raised his eyebrows. 'Awkward, but I expect it's an occupational hazard if you decide to share. Monastic bliss for me. I've got some groovy ideas for a bachelor pad.'

'Do you like being a bachelor?'

'Up to now.' He smiled at her, and she rushed on, 'I imagine you would have plenty of groovy ideas.'

'Why?'

'Well, I hear on the grape-vine you've introduced a few of them in the firm so I don't expect it would stop at five-thirty. You being creative, I mean.' She smiled at him.

'So are you.' He looked around again, 'What a good idea to choose beige and orange as a background for your dark beauty.'

'Shucks.'

'I can remember you coming to our school dances.'

She didn't believe him. 'I was unrecognisible then, a pudding. I hadn't the strength of will to refuse stodge.'

'You obviously have now.' His glance was admiring, took her in from head to toe. Was the black dress too low?

'That's worry.'

'What are you worried about?'

'That I'm twenty-six and not married.' The words came out without thinking. To her dismay she blushed, a painful, ugly blush. Even her armpits stung. She got up quickly, too embarrassed to sit still.

'Where are you going?' She must look a sight. Even the way she had jumped to her feet had been ungainly.

'To get a handkerchief.' She went quickly into her bedroom leaving the door open in her haste, and when she sat down on the stool in front of the dressing-table she saw that he was leaning against the jamb of the door.

'Kate,' he said, 'you were blushing.'

'All right, I was blushing.' She met his eyes in the mirror. 'Now I am putting on some powder to cover my blushes.' She banged a puff against her cheeks. 'I must have touched a raw, bleeding nerve or something. Most of the time I'm thankful not to be married. I lead a full and interesting life. I travel a lot. I would be a dead loss as a wife.'

'Don't denigrate yourself.' He came behind her, and when she got up hurriedly she found she was in his arms.

'What the hell do you think you're doing?'

'Kissing you. Do you mind?' He took a long time over it. Her body responded to his. She pulled herself away before it became too obvious.

'I do admit we come from the same place,' she was still nervous, too silly, 'and that we probably danced together on one of those ghastly occasions when we were ferried over so that the little boys could have a feel at the little girls, but,' she tried to smile, 'I don't think it gives you any territorial rights.'

13

'I just wanted to.' He was disarming, 'Isn't that a good enough reason?'

'For old times' sake? All right, but don't make a habit of it.' She walked quickly into the sitting-room, was relieved that he followed her. Talking to him with her bed, a large one, looming behind them, had been difficult. She hadn't wanted to look at it in case he thought it was an invitation.

Here she could be at ease, fill up his glass, turn on some more lights, feel momentarily gratified that the sand colour and tangerine made a good background for her, as were the jewel blue cushions, as was the Pollock, although it was too smooth, too print-like, well, it *was* a print. Who could afford the real thing?

'I used to cycle to school,' she said, smiling at him, feeling completely herself now. 'The times I had flat tyres, the times I pushed that bike up hills! I must have had leg muscles like a prize fighter.'

'I don't go back to Cheltenham often now. I've an aunt there but my parents are both dead.'

'Oh, I'm sorry!' She felt a quick stab of sympathy. And I've still got two, she thought, I could share them with you, Mum and Dad would be delighted, a home town boy, local boy made good.

'I've a sister in Scotland. Married.' He was looking at his watch. 'I think we'd better make tracks. It's Wimbledon, isn't it?'

'Yes, but they've got a country house in Dorset. Somewhere near the sea. You'll probably be invited there too. Lead on, then.'

She went round the flat putting off lights. When she had pressed the switch at the door and he was standing beside her in the darkness she wondered if he would kiss her again, but he didn't try. She was disappointed. That's what you get for being greedy, she thought.

14

Lawrence came into the hall with Kate. Their coats were taken from them and Kate shook her head smilingly when the woman asked her if she would like to go upstairs. He was amused how she pushed her hand through her hair once, and smiled at him. 'Too late to do anything about me now.' He thought that she should not denigrate herself so much, while he realised that there was a pocket of unsureness somewhere. Was it because she was unmarried at twenty-six? It was no age nowadays. He felt warmly towards her. One could do a lot worse . . .

They took their place in the queue which stretched ahead of them into a room at the top of the hall. It would look out on to the garden. He had noticed the shaven lawns, the flowering shrubs, the effect of careful attention which both the garden and the house gave. And plenty of money.

He whispered to her, 'Gracious living. All the trimmings.' Grant does himself well, he thought. Who said publishing nowadays didn't pay? There was even some kind of major-domo announcing the guests. Everyone chatted softly, trying not to look impressed.

'Miss Henderson and Mr. Paton.' He didn't mind being paired with Kate. She looked marvellous tonight. Pretty, and yet the intelligence shone through. Anyone could do a lot worse . . . Hadn't he thought that before?

'Lawrence! Good to see you. My wife,' Grant was saying, 'I don't think you've met.'

'How do you do.' Formidable, he said to himself, the French way.

'And Julia.

And Julia. She was holding out her hand, a tall girl so slight that her body seemed to sway forward with the hand. 'Hello,' she said. She had a glorious smile and yet the little lift of her head made him feel that she was embarrassed to be the cause of all this fuss.

'Hello.' He found he was completely tongue-tied. Kate was filling in the gap. Saying just the right things. 'Everything looks marvellous. It must have meant a tremendous amount of work.'

'Yes, I feel . . . terribly responsible.' The girl shook her head, the glorious smile again.

'You look lovely. Lovely dress . . .'

The talk buzzed, there must have been an instant camera in his head, because now that they had moved on he found that his memory was completely photographic, as if he was looking at a tear-off. In colour. The pale hair which swung forward as she held out her hand, the awkward little gestures which tall girls often have, the intense blue of her eyes, the eyelashes which looked and therefore must feel like fur, thick and soft. The motif is gold, he thought, pale gold skin, pale gold hair, lashes dipped in gold paint. The broad brow, the fine nose, the short upper lip, he saw them all clearly, even the terrible dress like a chocolate box lid.

She's just a blonde blue-eyed girl, his common sense said, they come in their thousands, most blondes are dark-heads anyhow, dissatisfied with their lot. But this one wasn't. She was blonde through and through, the hair-line was blonde, even the skin of her hands was the real blonde skin, paper-fine, shell-like . . . he saw that Kate was chatting to some people she knew and he was glad of the respite.

An absurd memory came back to him of his sister, Grace, lifting carefully from its box a Christmas doll, and how the perfection of it made him want to hold it. 'Don't touch,' she said, 'it's not for little boys.'

Too perfect? One had been trained, possibly through modern novels, certainly by fashion, to view with suspicion beautiful blonde girls, there was a connotation of silliness somewhere, one thought of the classic dumb blonde. But Julia wasn't like that, although she hadn't spoken much. Her face had been animated, her eyes had followed Kate intently, she gave the impression of a nervous intelligence, of sensitivity, of too great a vulner-

16

ability for twenty-one. He saw again the lancing forward of the tall, slender body, the pale hair slipping over the wide forehead . . .

'He's in a dream,' Kate was saying. 'Lawrence, this is Jane and Arthur Bayliss, co-authors, they do everything together.'

'Oh, hello,' he said, 'great to meet you. I love your stuff.' He spoke rapidly, launching into a discussion with Bayliss about the technique behind who-dunnits . . . beautiful, beautiful . . . the word was being repeated inside his head as he queried, suggested . . . I've never seen anyone so beautiful. . . .

2

'You've been hiding from me all evening,' Lawrence said. 'Would you like to dance?'

'Yes, please. And I haven't been hiding from you, I've been hoping you'd ask me for ages.'

'Honestly?'

'Honestly.' Her blue eyes so near his face gave him a feeling of dizziness. He was glad to draw her against him so that her face was hidden against his shoulder. 'I'm so glad it's a smoochy one,' he said.

'Why?' Her voice was muffled.

'Well, I'd rather dance like this than cavort in front of you. I'm getting too old for that.'

'What age are you?' She came away from him. 'Everybody knows my age tonight. It's only fair I should know yours.'

He laughed. 'Twenty-eight.'

'I thought you might be that.' She nodded and put her face against his shoulder again.

They danced without speaking and he marvelled at her

lightness. There's no girl here at all, he thought, her waist is incredibly thin, and this terrible dress is boned or something, like a paling round her softness. 'I like your dress,' he said, hoping she would look at him.

She did, and he noticed again the intense blueness of her eyes. The cheek which had been against his shoulder was flushed, the other one was pale. It made her look childlike. 'Do you really like it?'

To his dismay his eyes faltered, and he laughed to cover up, 'Well, it's very suitable for a twenty-first birthday girl, I should say. A fairy princess.' He didn't like that much.

'I wanted something trendy, a doing-your-own-thing kind of dress. Bits and pieces. Or soignée, like Miss Henderson's. It's absolutely right for her.'

'Everyone should dress the way they want to.' He felt this conversation about dresses had gone on far too long.

'I leave it to my mother. She has excellent taste.' She sounded as if she was quoting.

'What do you care about?'

She swayed back over his hand on the small of her back. Her eyes were wide, intent. 'What do I care about?' She hesitated, 'What do I call you? I didn't hear your name. It sounds rude not to say it.'

'Would Lawrence do?'

'I like that. Do you know, Lawrence, I lay in bed this morning wondering what I should care about. There are so many puzzles, it's difficult . . .'

'That's half the fun.'

'I can see it would be to you. You square up to things. You never will have to ask yourself questions.'

'What kind of questions?'

'Who am I? That kind of thing. Sometimes you feel that some ordinary trivial thing is going to give you the answer, for instance, this morning there was a chair against the window . . . What was it you asked me?'

'I asked you what you care about?' And that's an odd

18

question to be asking, he thought. But somehow, with this girl, he was forced to take up attitudes, make remarks which were unlike him . . .

'I sculpt a bit, well, model, really. I care about that. But that sounds very important for what I do, mangle clay. Do you know who I feel like sometimes?' She laughed, 'You'll never believe it. Michelangelo. His unfinished stuff, I mean. The way he *drags* the thing out from the stone. Mine are all unfinished. That's the only resemblance. I'm pretty hopeless.'

'I'm sure you're not. Perfectionists always think that of themselves. Where do you work?'

'I don't work.'

'I mean sculpt.'

'At St. Martin's sometimes. Not so often now. I've got an attic upstairs. I like attics particularly. You see the branches of the trees and you can forget you're in Wimbledon outside London, you can make your own place Sometimes I think I'm Igraine in Tintagel castle, I rea about her the other day. At Tintagel the gales wou howl round you and the waves would slap against t stone . . . other times I imagine it's one of those lov peaceful châteaux in France, the one with the bridge o the water, so that when you're in the great hall you water from every window . . . that's the beauty of trees, you can imagine anything.'

He hid his surprise. 'Don't you find it lonely?'

'In what way?'

'Well, most girls of your age like company. I s that's why they flock to offices and then they ha little natters about that upstart Lawrence Pat what the boyfriend said last night and how man tights they've ruined that week.'

'I like company, but sometimes I feel it do me. Girls never seem to talk like that to me, an have a run of shopping trips and lunche mother, I get a terribly impatient kind of fe like a criminal wasting time. That it wasn't given to us for that.'

'I'm an inveterate time-waster.' He laughed at her.

'I don't believe you.' She seemed uncomplicated again. 'Father says you're a find and that you can draw rings round the rest of the directors. I heard him tell Mother that when you walked away.'

'You'll make me blush.'

They had reached the corner where the group were playing. She stopped and he kept his arm round her thin waist. She spoke to the leader, 'That's a marvellous number. I really loved it. What's it called?'

' "Mood Indigo", Miss Fairfield. Duke Ellington.'

'It's really atmospheric. I truly loved it. Do you think we could have a loud knockabout one now, never mind if you bring the roof down.'

'All right, suits me,' he stroked his silk hair, 'but you must take the blame with Mr. Fairfield. Okay,' he said, turning to the group, 'Huckleberry.'

The immediate noise crashed on their ears and Lawrence pretended to fall back. She laughed at him. 'Can't you take it? Don't you like it?' She began to sway in front of him, wreathing her arms above her head.

The sighing lady in the embattled tower had disappeared. It was difficult to keep up with her. When she moved she moved like a smoke drift, when she danced in front of him she rolled and shook her head, revolving it on her shoulders so that the pale gold hair was tossed about and had a life of its own. Her face emerged through it, flushed, laughing. 'Do you like it, Lawrence?'

'Love it.' He was doing his best. 'There's only one thing you've got to promise.'

'What's that?'

'That you'll come and sit on the stairs with me after we've had a long cool drink. My legs won't hold me up much longer.'

From then on he monopolised her. He was probably

20

rude. Occasionally he felt guilty about Kate, but when he did and he searched her out with his eyes, he saw that she was having her own not inconsiderable success with other men.

But Julia . . . with her head resting against the staircase and the long white throat extended and those blue eyes on him. Flushed cheeks, like a child who has been allowed up too late. She drank the champagne like water. 'Tell me about your job, Lawrence. Do you like books? I do. I keep searching in books. Do you like Blake? Do you know the lovely poem about the little black boy? I know it all. The ending . . . "and then I'll stand and stroke his silver hair, and be like him, and he will then love me".' She breathed deeply. 'The poignancy . . . asking for love. Everyone wants to be loved. Do you ever think you might write a book yourself? I feel I might, on the days when the clay's gone all to hell.'

He laughed at her, feeling slightly drunk. 'I don't know why you have me around. You're answering all your own questions.'

'No, I don't know any answers.' She shook her head solemnly at him, 'Would you like to come up to my attic and see my workroom?'

'I'd love to, but,' he looked around, 'you're the belle of the ball. Should you?'

'I've been very good for days about being the belle of the ball. I've even let them dress me up. It won't take long.'

He took her hand as they climbed the stairs. She staggered a little when they reached the second landing, and he put his arm round her shoulders. 'Steady.' He thought she leant against him, but with a featherweight you couldn't be sure.

When she pushed open the door and switched on the light he had lost all interest in the workroom and thought only of her. But, nevertheless, he was surprised. Some of the heads were good, very good. There was one of her mother which caught the confident lift of her head.

'Did your mother sit for you?'

'Oh, no, it's from memory. A girl would know every feature of her mother, wouldn't you think? So often she has to look at her mother's face when she's saying, "Now, Julia, if I were you . . ." ' She stopped abruptly.

There were some of children with the same short upper lip as her own. 'Who are they?' he asked.

'Me. I remember me when I was small.'

'You don't, you know.' He felt a maudlin tenderness, cautioned himself.

'I do. I know exactly what I looked like. Sometimes I was outside looking on. Do you know the feeling? I had a little friend called Crawford North and I often watched us playing together. We were so sweet. The grandparents thought so.'

'You're teasing.'

'Yes, I'm teasing. I'll tell you a secret.'

'Are you sure you want to?'

'Yes, to prove to you that I'm grown-up. Once Father and Mother and I were travelling through France and we stopped at Perpignan. Do you know it?'

'Yes, I had some marvellous Crème Chantilly there once.'

'Well, it was the fourteenth of July, you know how French people go mad about it, and after dinner we wandered about the town watching the fireworks. Everybody was dancing. It was very gay. I longed to dance, but Mother was bored and I kept on saying, "Just a little longer, please, just a little longer . . ." But she got cross with Father, although I knew it was really me, and said she was tired and we must all go to bed because we were having an early start in the morning. We were going to Spain.'

'I know,' he said, 'you're going to tell me you made an assignation with a Frenchman.' He was slightly uneasy, wanted to joke.

22

'That's nearer than you think. When I got up to my room I couldn't sleep. It was at the front of the hotel and it was filled with beautiful colours as the fireworks went off. Do you know what I did?'

He shook his head.

'I slipped down into the crowd again. When we had been standing watching the fireworks in the tower, it's at the end of a canal which runs through the town, we had chatted to an American. My father is very affable. This American had white teeth and a beard which is unusual for an American, isn't it?'

'Which? The beard or the white teeth?'

'The beard.' She smiled at him. 'And he had a white jersey with blue stripes round the neck and the sleeves.'

'Which you could see very clearly?'

'How did you guess?'

'Because you were on the outside looking on.'

'Well, I met him again and he said, "Have you escaped?" I wanted to laugh, it sounded as if I was under lock and key, but I said, no, I couldn't sleep. We walked along by the canal away from the fireworks and found a little café which was built on a bridge. He was very engaging. He made me laugh a lot.'

'I'll bet. How long were you out?' He heard his voice, sharp, almost querulous.

'Oh, only about half an hour. He tried to make me stay longer but I suddenly got worried in case Mother might go into my room to talk to me, she sometimes does that. She comes and sits on my bed and hasn't anything to say. Sometimes she says, "Have you anything to tell me, Julia? Anything?" I feel I want to make up things to please her. Anyhow, this American . . . we ran most of the way back to the hotel, we were laughing a lot. When we got there, he wasn't laughing any more. He said . . .'

'Come on, then, let's have the dirt.' He was suddenly furiously angry.

She looked at him. 'Nothing, he said . . . nothing. I said

23

goodbye and went upstairs and that was it. But I was excited. I didn't want to go to sleep for ages.'

He breathed deeply. 'You've been teasing me.'

'Yes, I've been teasing you.' She took his hand. 'Come and see my branches.'

There was a wide sloping window and they stood under it. The branches were black across it and the sky had a luminous quality although there was no moon.

'Isn't it lovely?' she said. 'Don't you agree? You could be absolutely anywhere. You could be absolutely anybody. For a boy, you could be on the deck of a sailing ship.'

'You don't get branches there.'

'A mast is a tree. That's the point of it. It can be absolutely anywhere, anybody. Choose someone.'

'D'Artagnan.' He pretended to stroke a moustache.

'Yes, that's good. D'Artagnan.' She looked at him.

He warned himself. Once, twice, but it was no good. Blame it on the champagne. He put his hands on her shoulders and turned her to face him. 'You're a strange girl, Julia.'

'Not strange,' her head was back on her shoulders, the blue eyes almost black, 'I don't want you to think I'm strange. I'm like other girls, really.'

'Are you?' He bent towards her, 'Well, other girls would expect . . .'

'I find you very gentle, Lawrence.'

'I'm not a bit gentle.'

'Do you want to kiss me?'

'Oh, Julia!' He felt callow, unsure, now his damned legs were trembling. He pulled her towards him, blaming it on the champagne.

He was surprised at her passion, and at the strength in her thin hands. Even Kate, who had been annoyed at her body's response earlier on, one could tell, hadn't shown anything like this. When he let her go she was breathing quickly and her eyes looked frightened. 'Don't blame yourself,' she said, 'it was me.'

'Oh . . . girl!' Looking at her, swamped in the ridiculous, encumbering dress, at her slightness, at the childish short upper lip, the awkward, thin hands hovering, there was a disparity . . . 'I think we'd better go down now,' he said.

'Yes, we'd better.' Her shoulders seemed to hunch. The bones pushed blue-white and polished against the paper-thin whiteness of her skin. The strapless bodice of the dress looked too big. She pulled at it, her head drooped, and the fall of hair closed like a door over her face. He kept his arm round her waist as they went downstairs, but she was unresponsive.

You're a hell of a fellow, he said to himself, bussing two women in one night. He couldn't understand why his legs were still trembling.

'Did you enjoy yourself?' he said to Kate, as he was driving her back to South Kensington.

'Tolerably.' Her voice sounded amused. 'I didn't see much of you, or rather, when I did you were with Julia.'

'Oh, that!' He tried to dismiss it lightly. 'She looked so damned pathetic in that great dress . . .'

He saw himself in the attic, Julia's face lifted to the window. 'Isn't it lovely? You could be absolutely anywhere . . .' He experienced again the sharp impact her beauty had made on him. and even more the, what was it, *poignancy* which went with it. Sadness. Why was she sad? On the face of it she had everything material she wanted. Her mother, who might be trying at times, wasn't an ogre, Grant was jolly, a good chap. No flair, but his experience in publishing made up for it . . .

'Did you know,' Kate said, 'that it's very dangerous to drive and let your mind wander? Sometimes the car does too and then you're in deep trouble.'

'Gosh! Was I? Only for a second, though. We're almost at your flat.' He changed down, looked in his mirror and drew into the pavement. 'One very charming, absolutely honest lady delivered safely home.'

'Would you like to come up for a drink as a just reward?' Her voice hesitated a little, and he found that engaging.

Yet he didn't want to go. He wanted to get home and lie in bed and think of that young girl, Julia Fairfield, rather gauche, ruminative, but you had to admit the beauty, that shy young thing who had slipped out of her bed in the middle of the night (not quite, perhaps) to meet a strange American. . . .

'Would you mind if I don't, Kate? I'd simply love to but I've got an early start tomorrow. I've to get over to Paris at the crack of dawn to see that friend of Parmentier's who has offered to translate his new book. I'll have to sleep off the champagne which was quite potent.'

'So I noticed.' It wasn't snide. He thought he knew her well enough for that, but it did suggest that his behaviour had been noticeable, and perhaps rude.

'I got embroiled,' he said. 'Every time I looked for you you were having the time of your life.'

'There's no need to apologise. You weren't responsible for me.'

'Good.' He jumped out and went round to open the door for her. 'Got your key?'

'Yes.'

'Okay, then.' He bent forward with the idea perhaps of kissing her cheek, but she now had her head down while she rooted about in her bag. The kiss skidded off her cheek and landed on her left ear. It wasn't a very satisfactory performance, considering his earlier one in her bedroom.

When she had put her key in the door she turned to him and said, 'Thanks a lot for ferrying me, Lawrence,' the 'ferrying' was subtle, and held out her hand.

3

'Do you think it was a success, Grant?' Lydia sat at the dressing-table brushing her hair with short decisive strokes. She thought she looked old in the mirror, there was a slight swelling beneath her eyes which might be bags before long. Soon be fifty, no longer able to pretend...

Grant was already installed in bed with a book. He made it a point to read, or at least skim through, their own publications. He thought he could tell by the appearance of a book in print whether it would be a success or not, regardless of the content. He looked up. 'Everybody was most complimentary and Julia looked bright and happy. I don't know why you go on about her sometimes.'

'I don't go on about her, Grant.' She stopped brushing to face him. 'It's just that she's so . . . different! Look at the young people who were there tonight and yet she didn't speak to them much. The Latham boys have turned out very well, and then there was Jonathan Peel. He used to have riding lessons with Julia, couldn't keep his eyes off her.'

'Julia is unsure of herself. People like that generally feel better with someone older. Which reminds me, she seemed to be in Lawrence Paton's company quite a lot.'

'Yes, I noticed that.' Of course she had noticed it, and also that they had disappeared for a time. She thought, when she saw them dancing, that Julia had looked flushed and excited. She had tried to pump her ten minutes ago, sitting on the bed in the pretty room with its white-painted furniture. Why did one think forever of white in connection with Julia? 'Just to say good night,' she had said. She had a recurrent picture of Julia and she having long, cosy, feminine chats which never seemed to come off. 'Did you enjoy your party, Julia?'

'Yes, Mother. It was absolutely marvellous.' Her cheeks were flushed, and she saw her daughter dispassionately for a moment and her undoubted beauty.

'Who did you dance with?'

'Lots of people, really. Father's friends, they were very sweet to me, Jonty Peel once or twice and some of the other young people but they seemed to form a clique . . .'

'Perhaps that was because you deserted them.'

'Deserted them? Oh, do you mean . . . ?' Her cheeks were hectic with the blush. Lydia felt sorry for her, tried to make her voice sound amused.

'Well, I did see you with that charming young director who came along with Kate Henderson. Lawrence, Paton, isn't it?'

'Oh, yes, Lawrence . . .' She saw clearly that Julia was struggling for composure. If she would only say something simple like 'Have a heart, Mother . . .' 'Yes,' she was saying, diffidently, 'Yes, we did spend some time together. We found we had a lot in common. He's very . . . sympathetic.' She looked at the counterpane. 'He has a nice smile,' then, shyly, her eyes searching Lydia's face, 'the kind of smile you could warm your hands at.'

She thought, how fanciful. 'You liked him?'

'Yes, I liked him.' The girl hesitated, and then said in a little rush of words, 'When we disappeared for a bit that was because I was showing him my heads. He seemed interested.'

'You don't have to account for every moment of your time, Julia. After all, you're twenty-one now.'

'Yes.' They smiled at each other and Julia said, 'You're good to me, Mother. Don't think I don't appreciate it. The lovely party, all the arrangements, the expense, I want you to know how much . . ."

'You don't have to make a speech about it,' she had said, more as a joke, but strangely enough Julia had gone silent and she too had been bereft of words. It had suddenly become embarrassing to sit on the bed. 'Well, sleep soundly,' she had said, getting up, 'good night, darling.'

Now she sighed, playing with her rings and bracelet. 'I'll put these away tomorrow. Hope we don't get burgled, but, suddenly, I'm very tired.'

'Come to bed, darling.' Grant didn't lift his eyes from his book. 'You've had a very busy day.'

She took off her dressing gown and got in beside him. 'You know what's going to happen,' she said. 'We're both tired out but we aren't going to sleep. Do you think we should each take a sodium amytal and give up trying?'

'No, not yet. Find yourself a book and we'll read for a bit.' He seemed immersed in his.

Lydia lifted one she was reading from the table beside her, an *avant-garde* offering by a youth of twenty-three who had packed a lot into his life, having collective highs, getting it on dex, going on acid trips. She felt it her duty to read it so that she should be forewarned, but the excessive self-preoccupation bored her.

Now if Julia were really sensible she would give up this ridiculous playing about with clay, shutting herself up for long hours on her own, refusing invitations from the young people whom Lydia and Grant had acquired for her by a fairly substantial outlay of money. The only thing she had made anything of was driving, and Lydia privately thought it was a fluke that she had been passed by the examiner. Her looks must have captivated him.

With her tiredness her sense of injustice increased. With Julia's looks and background she could have been out in the world, meeting some important kind of man. If she had been a secretary it could have been her boss, if she had been cooking directors' lunches (a job which she had once been offered), it could have been one of the directors.

But, no, nothing but that damned clay which got into her nails and made her hands look as if she was doing housework all day long. The usual nagging obsession filled her mind. I just can't understand her . . . so soft and gentle in some ways, so matter-of-fact in others. I can't get through to her . . . her tired brain resuscitated past irritants. The time when she, Lydia, had been afraid of the moth in her room, and how Julia, in answer to her call, had come in and had calmly caught it, keeping it a fluttering prisoner between her hands. 'Take it away, Julia,' she had implored, but she had smiled. 'I can't understand why you don't like them, Mother, they're pathetic, so pathetic, beating against my hands. Poor moth . . .' Why should that irritate her?

'Grant?'

'Mmmh?'

'Do you remember that time we stayed in Perpignan?'

He looked at her uncomprehendingly.

'Remember it was the 14th July and we watched the fireworks for a time?'

'Oh, yes, dear, yes, that was rather good fun. I say, this bloke is rather good, retired naval commander, but a gift of the gab all right . . .'

'Julia was with us. Lovely evening, mild. We didn't need jackets or anything. Do you remember I got tired and we went up to bed and Julia was silent because she had wanted to stay in the streets?' Give her her due, she thought, she's never been insolent in the whole of her life.

'Yes, I remember. Though I can't quite see why you are. It's quite natural for a young girl not to want to trail after her parents. What age would she be then? Seventeen? On the whole she's a very amenable girl, Julia . . .'

His eyes strayed longingly to his book and he was immediately immersed. There was no purpose in saying more.

Grant wasn't acute enough. He may have thought his daughter was amenable, but in reality that night she had been excited, her eyes had darkened, her cheeks were flushed, 'Good night, Mummy,' she had said, 'good night, Daddy.' There had been an aura . . .

And the next morning stains under her eyes, an air of fatigue, a something . . . she always came back to it. Saying to herself that she was doing her daughter an injustice didn't prevent her coming back to it, saying that mothers had notorious imaginations, saying that, all right, she would allow the basic jealousy . . . 'Would you like some tea, Grant?'

No answer.

'Grant?'

'Mmmh?'

'A cup of tea?'

He smiled at her. 'I knew you would get round to it. Pattern as before. What time is it?'

'Ten to three.'

'Well, it's just about tea-time.' He laughed, pecking at her cheek. 'Then around four you'll take that pill after all.'

'No, I won't. I'm trying to give them up completely.'

'And take tea-bags instead?' He returned to his book, chuckling.

The house was dark but it retained some of the warmth of the people who had thronged it. The caterers had cleared up in the hall, and there was no sign of their presence except that one of the Bukhara rugs was askew. She righted it with her foot.

She walked into the billiard room and saw that it was tidy too except that the gold chairs which had lined it were in orderly stacks waiting to be collected tomorrow. Beyond the French windows the garden looked peaceful. What a pleasant vista it was, she thought, illuminated by the light from the room, the smooth sweep of lawn rising to the rocky island planted with shrubs.

She realised she had a nagging headache. Too much excitement. She opened the catch of the window and stepped out on to the stone terrace. The urns were white on either side of the steps leading down to the lawn. Had Julia known, her dress was in a small way influenced by all this, a proper setting for a ballgown. Children laughed at most of one's ideas.

But it had been the wrong choice. She knew that now. The young in their motley dress had been right, as had the older group, exemplified by that charming girl from the office, Kate Henderson.

She turned to go back into the house, and looking up she saw that there was a light in one of the attics, Julia's workroom. She felt her cheeks flush with anger. She trembled as she went into the kitchen and put the kettle on to boil. It was really too bad of her. Why was she so annoying? She spoke to herself as she measured tea into the pot.

I, we, do everything for her, every blessed thing, and yet she will not *conform*. The next thing is she'll be taking up with awful people like the characters in that silly book I've been trying to read, getting stoned on grass. Even their vocabulary was meaningless. She really is a worry, I ought not to be worried like this.

On the stairs she hesitated with the tray and wondered if she could go up to the attic. And then dismissed the idea because she wasn't confident enough. The confrontation was too much for her, tired as she was. Besides, she reminded herself, the girl lives with you and Grant, don't forget, you at least *know* when her attic is lit, when she goes out or in.

'That silly girl is in her attic at this time of night,' she said to Grant. 'Really, it's too bad of her.'

Grant raised his eyebrows above his half-moons. 'Is she really?'

'Should I go up?'

'No . . . no, I don't think so. After all, you're cavorting about in the middle of the night too. It's been an occasion for her. She probably couldn't sleep either. It may be how she relaxes.'

'But if she couldn't sleep she could have come into us, she must have heard us talking, she could have sat on

the bed, and we could all have had a cosy cup of tea together . . .' She heard the whine in her voice. Give it up,
Lydia. You must accept the difference between what
you would like and what *is*. There's a fundamental lack
of rapport. You'll never experience it now. If it isn't there
by her twenty-first birthday it's no go.

It's a failure, but don't blame yourself too much. Give
yourself the credit for having tried . . . but it was no use.
The nagging obsession was still there. I'll never sleep, she
thought, I'm tired to death . . . Grant surprised her when
he spoke, taking off his glasses so that she knew he was at
last concentrating on her.

'Now that all the fun and games are over about this
dance, Lydia, I think you should have a bit of a rest.
You've had a great deal to do. How about going down
to the cottage for a week or so? I'll join you at the week-
ends, I might even manage a break in the middle of the
week.'

'I hadn't thought of it. I've got quite a few com-
mittees coming off . . .' But the idea appealed to her. She
thought of the cottage, of its long, low front, two
workmen's cottages made into one and then an extra
wing added, the door which was awry because of this,
and the French window which was awry because it had
been another door, the garden which was cottagey.
Corfe Cottage. They seldom gave it its full name.

Why couldn't they grow the same cottagey flowers
here? But, of course, it was the gardeners who were
different, here Bateson, who had once worked at Kew
and had formal ideas, there Jim Stopford from the
village who grew plants from packets of seeds in his
allotment. Then the earth was richer, and the air was
fresher . . . Grant surprised her again.

'I've another idea. Lawrence Paton, you know . . .'

'Yes?'

'I want to cultivate him a little. He's going to be very
valuable to us. He's got real flair. He thinks I've none,

but never mind about that. What do you say to me bringing him down the first weekend, that is, if he'll come. Shall I ask him tomorrow?'

'Or I could ring up?'

'No, it'll be more informal coming from me. Could you be bothered?'

Suddenly her depression over her failure with Julia vanished. What a good idea it was! He had been interested in Julia, and he was so very suitable, so very right, not too good-looking but with an air of confidence and good humour which was much more valuable.

How wonderful it would be if he had really fallen for Julia and they got married. They could have the wedding in Hanover Square, and, yes, the same caterers as they had had tonight, last night, but next time, organdi for the dress.

'Don't tell Julia,' she said, 'after all, he's a business associate and that's enough. Yes, I should invite him if I were you.' She tried to sound indifferent but when she lay down she felt happy and knew she would sleep.

4

Lawrence heard the tap on his door, and looked up to see Grant Fairfield. He smiled. 'Hello, come on in.'

'Sure I'm not interrupting anything?'

How handsome he looked, Lawrence thought, as he pulled forward a chair, grey and silver, grey suit, silver tie, silver side-burns, gleaming shirt. Of course Julia took her beauty from him, you could see it now, the regular features, although middle-age had taken the intensity out of the blue eyes. 'Take a pew,' he said.

'How are things, Lawrence?'

'Erratic. I'm honoured to have a visit from you.'

'I'm sure you don't think anything of the kind. You need have no reverence for my grey hairs.' But it was said with good humour and the usual chuckle. He seemed a happy man, uncomplicated. 'I looked for you in the office yesterday, but was told you had gone over to Paris.'

'Yes, I had to meet this friend of Parmentier's who's offered to translate his latest novel. Found her in a superior kind of hovel in Montmartre. Very intense. Seemed high to me, and I mean high.'

'Does Parmentier really want her?'

Lawrence considered. 'I'm not so sure about that. I imagine there's a question of past favours.'

'You don't seem too happy about it. Why don't you meet someone else? There's Gerry Susskind. He's been very successful recently with the *nouvelle vague* . . .'

'Yes, that's a good idea. I'd certainly like to.' He thought he must revise his opinion of Grant Fairfield, that his chuckling affability hid a more subtle mind than he had first thought. 'Let me say here,' he said, 'although it's got nothing to do with the subject that I had a marvellous time at your daughter's dance. You must have put a lot of work into it.'

'Not I, I leave it to Lydia. By the way, she would like very much if you could come down to our Dorset cottage this coming weekend if you're free. I'll arrange for Susskind to be there. He has a brother who lives near us. They're an extremely civilised family.'

'That's uncommonly good of you. I'd like that.' He hesitated. 'Will Julia be there?'

'Yes, I'm sure she will. I heard Lydia asking her this morning.'

'Perhaps it will be dull for her, meeting me again.'

'Since you're fishing,' Grant smiled at him, 'I can tell you that it would be the reverse. Lydia told her I would be asking you and she seemed pleased. There's no difficulty in knowing when she's pleased.'

'May I say you have a beautiful daughter?'

35

'Yes, you may, since everybody else does.' Lawrence's secretary came in with two cups of coffee and he waited until the girl had gone out of the room. He stirred slowly with his spoon. 'It's quite a handicap, beauty. So much more comfortable if they're just plain. They can disguise it fairly easily nowadays and, in any case, I think the plain ones marry quicker.'

'Perhaps. But you know what the poet says, "A thing of beauty is a joy for ever".' He thought he was now being really banal.

'Lydia thinks she should be conventionally fun-loving, shouldn't shut herself up half the day in that attic of hers.'

'She showed me her work. I thought it was good.'

'Yes, it's good, but it will never be good enough for Julia. I know her. I'll let you into a secret, Lawrence.' Something had loosened Grant's tongue. 'When I was young I was a bit of a recluse myself. In my case I was trying to write. I should probably have stayed like that, perhaps becoming more reserved, had my father not died suddenly and I had to go into the firm to keep the name going. Soon I had nothing but sympathy for poor authors who had to push the boat out, a page at a time, spinning words, really, it's quite ridiculously wearing when you come to think of it. Now I can enjoy reading them. I learned how to become an extrovert. I'm not a natural one, that's why I'm sometimes too fulsome.'

'You could have fooled me. Are there any natural ones?'

'I think you might well be.'

'Do you? Well, I hadn't given it any thought.'

'Which makes it all the more certain.'

He laughed. 'Perhaps you're right.'

'You're lucky that you're an extrovert with a flair which is quite the best combination. But unlucky because you haven't got the equipment to fully understand an introverted personality . . . Goodness me,' he

36

looked at his watch, 'I must have bored you to tears. Excellent coffee.' He put down his cup. 'I must get on with some work. I'm concerned at the moment with a jolly naval commander, not an *avant-garde* French writer. So I may count on you at the weekend?'

'Absolutely delighted. I'll drive you down if you like.'

'No, thanks, come under your own steam, if you don't mind. Then if you get too bored with us you can make a quick getaway. I'll give you directions later. Corfe Cottage, the place is called. Ten miles out of Dorchester. Wynbrook, just a hamlet, really. It was my people's place.'

'Okay. I've enjoyed our little talk.'

'Me too.'

He sat at his desk without moving after Grant had left him, trying to understand his rising excitement. Am I falling in love with this girl? Surely not. Only a few days ago I was immensely attracted by Kate Henderson. I was looking forward with pleasure to taking her to that dance, and what might follow, what I *started* in her flat . . . but since meeting Julia she's been there in my mind, in the plane going to Paris, walking along the Left Bank looking for bargains, there are none nowadays, just porn . . .

It wasn't her beauty, although anyone would enjoy looking at her. It wasn't her artistic talent, talented girls were ten a penny. What was it? Her poignancy, perhaps, her overwhelming need to be loved, to give love. A strange girl. She didn't want to be thought strange. She wanted to conform. But she was different, and in her difference lay her charm . . . the telephone rang and it was Kate.

'Back safely?' Utterly casual, no party hangnails.

'Safe and sound.'

'Did you fix things up?'

'Not quite. Grant has just been in and he wants me to meet Susskind. Do you know him?'

37

'Yes, he's very sound. A Jew. Charming.'

'I've been asked down to the Fairfields' cottage this weekend. I'll meet him there.'

'What did I tell you?'

'Did you?' He laughed, changed the subject. 'What can I do for you?'

'I'm trying to make amends for my feminine behaviour the other night.'

'Well, you are feminine, aren't you, unless you're hiding something from me.'

She laughed. 'I've a friend, Richard Lewis, a doctor, strangely enough his home is in Cheltenham too. Did you know him? He'll be about your age. No, twenty-six. Mine.'

'Oh, well, then, I wouldn't. At school we didn't speak to anyone in a lower form.'

'Filthy prigs. Well, Richard has come as a junior partner to a firm of doctors in South Ken, and he's got a flat very near yours and mine. Isn't it cosy? He isn't married. Why I don't know, because he's gregarious.'

'Perhaps he's trying to win you.'

She laughed, but he had a feeling that his remark had struck home. 'He's having a little drinks party on his day off, and he's asked me to be hostess. Am I being terribly long-winded?'

'No, I find this recital absolutely enthralling. Say on.'

'Well, would you like to come said she flatly.' She laughed. 'It's tonight.'

'Yes, I'd like to.'

She seemed taken aback. There was a pause, then, 'Okay. Here's the address. Ten, Marlborough Mansions. First floor.'

'Shall I call for you?'

'No, I'll be there early. I'm taking some bits and pieces for the party.'

'I should think that if you get to the point of making bits and pieces for a man it's as good as settled.'

'What nonsense! Richard and I are like brother and sister. Almost.'

'Almost? Is that the honest lady talking? Must get on, Kate. I've got masses to do. I'll be there. Thanks for asking me.'

'Six-thirty.'

'Fine. See you.'

Lawrence liked Richard Lewis immediately. He was ruddy-faced, curly-haired. The hair was recalcitrant. It had been obviously sleeked down at the sides, but the back turned up in a little riot of curls, probably the bane of his existence. Kate was beside him, satisfactory in black trousers and a gaudy top.

'Nice to meet you,' Lewis said. 'So glad you could come. Kate's been singing your praises.'

'Have you, Kate?' He looked at her and he thought she blushed faintly.

'To a certain extent. I said that you were clever but conceited, good-looking but that you knew it, going places but climbing on other people's shoulders to get there.'

'What a diatribe!' He laughed, but he felt vaguely annoyed.

'She castigates those whom she loves,' Lewis said. 'I've a feeling that if she said I had an ugly mug, well, an uglier mug than I have, and was a menace to the medical profession, I might get her to marry me. I've been trying for years.'

'Oh, men!' Kate said. 'I must circulate with these.' She had a plate of canapés in her hand.

'When did you move in?' Lewis asked. 'Kate says you're a new bug too.'

'About a week ago.'

'A week ago? I was lucky getting a flat. Kate told me about it. It's very handy for the surgeries.'

'Have you been in general practice long?'

'No, I'm a complete tyro. Keep it dark.'

'You've spilled the beans to the wrong fellow. I was going to ask you to become mine. I lived on the other side of the city, so I shall have to change doctors.'

'Bring your card round by all means. But you look so healthy that I'm sure you'll never need my services, which is all to the good.'

'Except for cover for the odd spot of malingering.'

Lewis laughed. 'I was in psychiatry before but I couldn't take it.'

'Where were you?'

'In a private place in Dorset. Dr. Susskind runs it. Have you heard of him? He's well regarded in the field, has written a good textbook.'

'No, I haven't, thank God. But I believe I'm meeting his brother at the weekend . . .'

'Yes, I've met him, Gerry.'

'But you couldn't take it?'

'No. There's something about the diseased mind which throws me, depresses me. It seems such a hell of a waste, then I get emotionally involved and I'm no use to the patient. There was a subtle infiltration. I found that I was becoming introverted like most of them. I got into the habit of spending my evenings in, I felt cut off, I *wanted* to feel cut off. And I can tell you . . . Lawrence, isn't it? I'm Richard . . . I can tell you, Lawrence, there's nothing makes you realise your own flaws quicker than being exposed to psychiatric cases. I felt I had to get out into the cut and thrust of ordinary existence again, the human jungle, even although it's general practice in London and I'll be up against the petty little complaints that most people plague your life with.'

'I promise not to come to you with any petty complaints.'

'Good. Come round any day and I'll sign you on. It's been great to talk to you but I must circulate a bit since it's my own party. Kate's being an angel.'

40

Lawrence spoke to Kate later. 'May I take you home, please, miss?'

She looked surprised and pleased. 'I've got my own car. I had to bring the stuff for the party. Sorry, but thanks all the same.'

'You Women's Lib lot! When is a man going to get you alone and unprotected for God's sake, with or without brassière?'

'A man has just to ask.'

'Well, then, how about it? We could go to the theatre if you like. What's your choice?'

'Anything goes for me, provided it's well done. Even the cinema.'

'The cinema has only skin-flicks now. I've never been a voyeur, I'm an up and doing man.'

'Yes, it's too boring . . .' She half-turned, a woman had put an arm round her. 'Oh, hello, Mary! And Gordon! I thought you avoided parties like the plague.'

The man had a bald head and a paunch but contrived nevertheless to look quite young. 'I'd go anywhere to meet you, sweet Kate.'

Lawrence moved away. He should have named an evening, been more definite, but something cautioned him. Don't get too involved. Wait until after the weekend, when you've seen Julia again. Julia . . . she was there again in his mind, had been there through the talk and banter, even when he had been interested in what Lewis was saying to him.

He left. And in the quietness of his own flat he thought of her, and when he was in bed which he had gone to quickly without a nightcap, and without taking some stuff to read out of his brief-case. The room seemed to be full of her, her delicacy and her child-like attitudes, her shyness, and then that was superseded by the fast-moving, head-rolling Julia who had danced in front of him . . . and from that he went to the Julia who had slipped out of her hotel when her parents were in bed.

41

And yet always there was the poignancy, the feeling that she needed someone, no, not someone, he, Lawrence, needed his strength. And his protection. That, banal as it might sound, they were meant for each other. For God's sake, he said, get to sleep.

In the early hours of the morning he got up out of bed, tired with thinking, and stood at the window, looking out. The street was quiet, the cars were parked on either side of it, the red-brick frontages of the blocks shone bone-white at the window edges. She needs me, he thought again, saying that if someone came along, at this moment, he would admit it, finally, that he had fallen in love.

Into his vision came a youth who walked unsteadily, stopped to lean against a car before he went on. Drink or drugs. But he had seen someone, it was a talisman, and he said, I am in love with her, deeply, basically, nothing to do with the short time they had known each other, nor their suitability for each other. I've got to tell her when I'm there, he thought, if I feel as badly as this I've got to tell her. See what she thinks of me. He remembered her kisses and thought she would not be indifferent.

5

'I like this kitchen almost better than the Wimbledon one,' Julia said. She looked around contentedly, her hands deep in a mixing-bowl. Lydia smiled, and she knew that she was making her mother happy, that this situation, that of mother and daughter working companionably together, was what she wanted.

'Yes, I know what you mean. The fitted units all look like magazine advertisements, whereas here there's much more character.'

'The Aga's comforting, real, live heat, this good big table . . .'

'What's that you're doing now?'

'The puff pastry for the game pie.'

'I can never get it right. I usually take the coward's way out and buy it ready-made.'

Julia laughed. It was so easy to please her if you tried. 'I remember getting the prize at Stanstead for making the best puff pastry. My hands are always cold. Perhaps that helps?'

'They say so. Where's the stuffing for the beef olives? I can be preparing them while you're finishing that.'

'In the frig. And have a look at the Pavlova. See that it hasn't collapsed.'

Lydia opened the refrigerator door and inspected the contents. 'I won't have a thing to do all weekend. Everything looks fine.'

We're both playing the game. Lydia turned, and Julia thought, here it comes. She can't leave it alone, she's going to tell me again about Rosemary Munro and how successful she's been . . . 'Do you remember Rosemary Munro at Stanstead, Julia?'

'Yes.'

'I met her mother the other day. Rosemary has gone into partnership with a friend and they've got a very successful little business now. They go out and cook special dinners. They get awfully well paid, and the beauty of it is that they can take on as little or as much work as they want.'

It hadn't been the other day, it had been quite three months ago, and this was the third time of telling. 'It would be boring eventually.' She rotated the pie dish on one hand as she spoke, cutting off the superfluous pastry with a deft movement of her knife. 'Think of the ruination of all your work, the horrible left-overs. You've nothing to show for it at the end.'

'Still, their own little business . . .' Julia, cutting

leaves of pastry, waited for her mother to say something about clay and the mess and the waste of time, but to her surprise she changed the subject. She spoke lightly. 'Where's the chicken, darling?'

'In the larder. I've got the liquor boiling. I'll do some saffron rice and then I think that's all.' She smiled at her mother, thanking her with her eyes, grateful that there had been no senseless arguments.

'Entertaining's always easier here somehow although we have much less help. Thanks for all you've done, Julia. I'll go and change now. Lawrence Paton will be here within the next hour. He's driving down alone.' She spoke almost absently, taking off her apron, hanging it up, but the name caused a swift stab of delight to run through Julia, like a painless kind of neuralgia.

'I'll rush up and tidy my room.'

Upstairs she sat on the unmade bed trying to calm herself. Everything had gone well. Mother and she were on good terms, her hair, which she had washed late last night, lay smoothly on her shoulders. Lawrence, she thought, Lawrence . . .

She walked about the room hugging her body with her arms, caught sight of her face in the mirror of the dressing-table and went over to peer at it. Her eyes had gone a much darker blue, she imagined her face glowed with some kind of inner light. He would be here soon. They would go for a long walk together, away from her father's affability, from her mother's watchful eyes and awkward questions. She would have him to herself.

She got up and went towards the wardrobe. She opened the door and looked at herself in the long mirror. No, she wouldn't change yet. Her trousers were fresh, pale blue linen, the blue shirt near her face deepened the blue of her eyes. She would carry her camel-hair sweater in case it grew cold. But it wouldn't grow cold. Not with Lawrence.

She heard a car draw up, scraping the gravel. She

44

crossed to the window and saw Lawrence getting out. He was wearing dark trousers and a light sweater and he looked trim and hipless as he went round to the boot and opened it. He took out his case, straightened and looked up, caught sight of her. 'Hello!' He waved.

'Hello.' The window was open, and she leant on the sill, feeling the stab of delight again, a deep-reaching thrust. 'You're early.'

'Too early?' Seeing his face at a new angle raised to her was interesting. She saw the wide brow foreshortened, the thickness of his hair round his ears.

'No, but Father's not here yet. He always travels by train. Mother will be leaving to pick him up in about . . .' she looked at her watch, 'ten minutes. Ring the bell and let her know you're here. I'll come down.'

When Julia reached the hall Lydia was talking to Lawrence. She was not at all flustered at his early arrival. She admired her mother's calmness while she felt her own heart knocking against her ribs.

'Here's Julia,' she said. 'I've just been complimenting Lawrence on his driving. He says he did it in under three hours.'

'That's good.' Her voice was rough and she cleared her throat. She wondered if she should shake hands but Lawrence only smiled at her and said, 'Hello again.' And to Lydia, 'She was hanging out of the window.'

'Only because I heard your car . . .'

Lydia looked at her. She couldn't tell if her mother was annoyed. 'I'm just going into the station to meet Grant.'

'Would you like me to do it?' Lawrence said.

'Not at all. Julia will entertain you until I come back. Won't you, Julia?'

'Yes.' She felt tongue-tied and then said, 'Did you see my car in the drive, Lawrence? It's the one I got for my twenty-first.'

'The Triumph Coupé? Very nice.'

'Julia and I drove down in it,' Lydia said, 'it gave her some practice. You've got to have one car here for shopping and getting to the sea. Grant won't bring his. He's childishly fond of a train journey. Well, I must go. Julia, show Lawrence to his room.' She smiled at him, 'Make yourself at home.'

When she had gone out of the door there was a small pause. Then Julia said, 'Would you like to go upstairs with your things?' She had wanted her mother to go, now she felt shy alone with him.

'Yes, please.'

'It's this way.' She went in front of him, acutely aware that he was only a step behind her.

He expressed admiration of the room. 'It's a real country bedroom,' and, crossing to the window, 'a real country view. Fields and more fields and then they disappear. What's in the hollow, Julia?' He turned to her where she was standing at the door. 'Come in. I won't eat you.'

She smiled and bit her lip, moving nearer to him. 'It's a place called Cuckoo Wood. I often go there. You've to climb a few stiles to get to it, but it's worth it. I keep a look-out for mushrooms if we're here in the autumn. Early morning's the best when there's dew. I'll show you the bathroom.'

He followed her out of the room and peeped briefly at the bathroom over her shoulder. 'Very adequate. I'll wash the London grime off and be downstairs with you in a minute.'

'Would you like me to make you some tea?'

'No, thanks. I don't drink it.'

'We're having people in for drinks at six-thirty. Can you wait until then for something?'

'Of course. I had a huge lunch.'

'Let me see. There's the vicar and his wife, Mother is always very countryish when she comes down here and includes them, and the Wards. Mrs. Ward is a friend of

Mother's in London too but she has the cottage at the end of the lane. It's where . . .' She stopped herself. 'Mother and Mrs. Ward go to matinées together. Then there's Mr. Susskind. He lives in London but he has a married brother who lives near here . . . I'll see you when you come downstairs.'

'All right.' He smiled at her and again the delight shook her and she wanted to hug her body again, to walk about, to run, to keep moving. She went downstairs and into the lounge, sitting primly on the chintz-covered chair at the door, but only for a moment, getting up and wandering about the room and then into the hall again. She met Lawrence.

'I've had a bright idea,' he said. 'I'd like to stretch my legs after driving. What about showing me Cuckoo Wood?'

She smiled, pleased at the idea. 'All right. I'll leave a note for Mother.' She went quickly to Lydia's desk in the lounge, found an envelope and wrote swiftly, 'Have taken Lawrence for a walk. Back soon.' She stuck it up on the mantelpiece, feeling important and somehow master of her fate.

Strangely enough, as they walked, the elation left her to be replaced by a steady kind of happiness which was even better. Lawrence made her laugh. He told her about his trip to Paris, and the Frenchman, Parmentier, mimicking his voice but sounding like Chevalier.

She said, 'That house at the end of the lane where the Wards are now . . . that's where Crawford North used to come to stay with his grandparents. Remember I told you about him before?'

'Your childhood sweetheart?'

'Well . . . You see *my* grandparents lived in our house so we were quite near to each other. It was they who added the wing to the original cottages. They stayed here all the time when they got old. They loved it.'

'What was this paragon of virtue like, Mr. Crawford

North?' He bowed in a ridiculous fashion, offering with spread hands to help her over a stile.

'No, I can get over myself.' She didn't want him to touch her. 'He was quick and dark-haired. He was good at everything. He could climb trees like a monkey. Once he climbed up a cedar in his garden, it's near the church, perhaps you noticed, and there are the same trees round them both. He was terribly high up. I remember thinking that he was going to climb right up into heaven. I was terrified and I ran home and sat in my room and prayed for him. Come down, Crawford, I prayed, come down, please come down . . .'

She stopped speaking because they were at the entrance to the wood and they had to jump over a small stream. He went first and held out his hands but she avoided them. When she had crossed they walked on, the sunlight dappling their faces and clothes. The heavy scent from the drifts of wild hyacinths under the trees was all around them. We could walk like this for ever, she thought . . .

'You've had some high old times with Crawford North,' Lawrence said suddenly. He smiled at her, and the tenderness of his smile made her want to weep.

'Yes. He was quite like you, actually, you're quick too, and he had a darting smile like yours.'

'You make me sound like a lizard.'

She laughed. 'You don't put your tongue out.'

They had come to a clearing in the wood with a fallen log lying across it. Clumps of late primroses pushed against the bark. 'We'll sit down here,' Lawrence said, 'I've got quite a lot to say to you.'

'Have you?' Her heart started to beat rapidly. She sat down, her hands on each side of her fingering the bark, pulling at it. It came away and she felt the sawdust going in behind her nails. Mother didn't like how she made a mess of her hands with clay, but when you handled natural materials like clay, or this wood, you hadn't to be

48

thinking of your hands, but your hands in relation to the material. You had to get the feeling of the material right inside you. She became excited at the thought of doing some wood carving. It would be finicky, of course, those small chisels, but you could polish it by rubbing it with your hands, over and over again, you could make a stoat, for instance, with a long smooth back which swept into a raised curve, and which had a small, lifted head.

'Julia,' Lawrence said, laughing at her, 'where are you away to now? Are you still with Crawford North?'

She met his eyes and thought she saw love in them. Or was it a reflection from her own? For she loved him. She crossed her hands in her lap.

He took her hands. He held them firmly in his. She had to look at him and again she thought he was like Crawford. There was that cleft at the side of his mouth which deepened when he smiled.

'Julia,' Lawrence said, 'I'm in love with you. It happened,' he lifted his shoulders, 'like that. I've thought of you a great deal. I wanted you to know. You don't have to do anything about it, just think about it, and then perhaps when you come back to town we could start seeing each other and you might grow to like, and then love me.'

Her heart was full. This was pain now. She lowered her eyes and felt the tears gathering at the back of them like a sluice waiting to be opened. But she mustn't weep. Lawrence wouldn't like girls who wept and behaved in a childish fashion. He would need a modern, mature girl like . . . like Kate Henderson.

'Have I offended you in some way?' She heard the tremor in his voice. The tears seemed to rush back from her eyes and bury themselves in her body, unshed.

'No . . . no, Lawrence. It just doesn't seem real. I've thought of you so much since my dance, I was sure that I had been . . . foolish, especially in the attic. I had too much champagne. I was still thinking of you in the

49

morning. Well, I came to the conclusion that since I was thinking of you so much I must love you. Don't you think so?' She raised her eyes to him, and he drew her into his arms, rocking her gently.

Behave, she admonished herself, don't throw yourself at him, don't frighten him with your elation, as you did before. He's Lawrence, important, Father thinks a lot of him, he'll want a cool girl, mature like . . . like Kate.

He pulled her to her feet and hugged her boyishly, almost exuberantly. She felt her feet leaving the ground for a second. They swayed back to smile and smile at each other until he laughed and pressed her face against his shoulder. 'I shan't harm you, Julia,' he said, 'I'll be very gentle.' She tried to listen to the wood noises as they stood, but she could hear nothing for the beating of her heart. 'I've never heard the cuckoo when I've been here,' she said, 'just on long, still summer afternoons in the garden it drifts across the fields, a sad note, really, very sad . . .'

'Damn!' he said, 'it's well after five.' She saw the gold bracelet for a moment on his wrist, black hairs. 'We'd better get back or your mother and father will think I've absconded with you.'

They held hands as they walked quickly back. At each stile he kissed her as he helped her over, but she remained calm and was loving but mature, so as not to frighten him. Men didn't like unbridled girls, she remembered Lydia once saying.

They got back to the house about six o'clock and she said to him in the hall, 'Go into the lounge. Mother and Father will be there. I'll have to go up and change.'

'Okay.' He pressed his fingers to his lips and then pressed them against hers. She saw the love in his eyes again. She wanted to cling to him in abandon. Instead she went quickly upstairs.

In her room she looked out and saw her car parked awkwardly in the middle of the drive. Mother must have rushed in quickly, expecting that Lawrence would be waiting for her. She would go down and put it in the garage. Thoughtfulness like that would please Mother, a conventional, daughterly thing to do, 'Mother, I put the car away to give more room in the drive . . .'

In any case, she couldn't keep still. The idea of lying motionless in a bath appalled her, or sitting quietly at her dressing-table. The elation was back in full force. Lawrence . . . She walked quickly once or twice across the room before she ran downstairs, out of the door, and got into the car. Good, the keys were in the ignition.

She didn't know how she found herself on the Dorchester Road rather than in the garage. Somehow when she had put her hands on the wheel she had felt such power coming out of her, running down her arms to the tips of her fingers, that she had had to go on driving. Just a little spin, of course. It would work off her excitement, calm her down, and then she would come back, get dressed, and make an entrance when all the people were there. It would be easier that way. At cocktail parties nobody ever noticed anyone coming in once they had got properly started.

At this time of the evening the light was golden. Peach golden. She saw it gild her bare arms, felt the cool air draw her hair back from her face. The road was striped like a tiger's back, she went in and out of the golden bars of light between the trees, it was like entering Paradise each time. Not many people on the road just now. All in drinking cocktails or having a farmhouse tea. Once she heard a cuckoo. Would it be from their wood? How sad it sounded, how old . . . some sounds were as old as the world . . .

It was a grand little car, this. Speed. Really, when you thought about it she was quite a good match for Lawrence. She could cook him directors' lunches and dinners, and she could drive into the station and pick him up in the evenings. He would look like a grown-up

Crawford North, a Crawford North with a bowler and the smile which was similar with the cleft at the side of his mouth. Not a dimple. The porter would say, taking his ticket, 'I think your wife is waiting for you, sir,' and he would look for her, turning his neck, and having seen her, smile . . .

He would be smiling just now, telling Mr. Susskind, or Mr. Barley, the vicar, about their walk. 'Julia and I may soon be getting married. We are eminently suited . . .' But he hadn't said anything about marriage, had he? Well, he would be talking anyhow. And smiling. He didn't have to say anything about their walk, it was a secret yet . . .

'It's a great pleasure meeting you,' Lawrence said, shaking hands with the Susskind brothers in turn. 'Now, let me get you straight.' He smiled at the two men.

'I'm Gerry,' the more obviously Jewish one said, 'pay no attention to Leo, he has enough admirers.' The other man smiled, and turned away to speak to someone who had touched his arm. Lawrence was left with the impression of dark eyes set importantly, in a woman they would have been called beautiful, and a dark face with a strong jaw.

'I've been looking forward to having a chat with you,' he said to Gerry. 'Are you interested in doing a translation of Parmentier's new novel? He's got someone lined up, but frankly I should like to have a choice.'

'I'd have to read it first. And if I decide to take it on, or if you decide to have me, I always insist on meeting the author. Besides, how else can I keep my expense account healthy?' He laughed.

'Could you let me see a sample of your work? Parmentier's friend has done the first three chapters. Could you do the same?'

'Yes, easily. Send it to me and then perhaps we can talk business.'

52

He looked around for Julia but didn't see her. 'It's a charming house this.' He pretended to be admiring, but was surprised at his impatience. He saw that the other brother had joined them again.

'I must apologise for rudely leaving you,' he said. 'Someone who had something important to say to me or thought it was important . . .'

'So what did I tell you?' Gerry said, 'they even follow him to cocktail parties!'

'Gerry, do me a favour and go and talk to some of those charming ladies.'

'Okay.' Gerry raised his hand in mock salute. Lawrence watched him for a second, then turned to his brother, smiling. 'Cocktail parties are good places to talk business.'

'Yes. It's not the first patient who's offered to strip for me.'

'You're in the right business for that. By the way, I met Richard Lewis the other day. I believe he worked with you for a time.'

'Yes, very successfully, but not, I'm afraid, as far as Richard was concerned. I was glad for his sake that he decided to give it up.'

'He's in a practice in London now.'

'Yes, I know. That's the life for him. He'll wear himself to a frazzle worrying about Mrs. Smith's back before he realises it's the same thing as he left.' He looked round the room again for Julia. Had she climbed into a bath and fallen asleep? Nothing would surprise him about Julia.

'I hear the daughter of the house is very beautiful,' Susskind said.

'Very.' He knew he reddened, and felt he must cover up. 'We had a walk together and then she went to change. I expect she'll be down soon.' He marshalled his forces, looked directly at Susskind. 'I was thinking the other day that normal people have a strong sense of their own identity. I suppose this is one sign of normality?'

'What is normal?' He spread his hands, shrugged. 'There's a new mode of thought which says that it is the *patients* who are normal. But I agree it's difficult for some people to think of themselves as part of a continuing process. They seem to live in some kind of existential vacuum . . .'

She felt like a bird. Like that seagull which had swooped above the little boy and girl on the beach. And, like the seagull, she could see the girl in the white car far below, her fair hair streaming behind her, a smile on her lips. She was a happy girl because Lawrence had told her he loved her, and that was fortunate because she badly needed someone to love her. The seagull beat the air with its heavy wings and then glided on a long sweeping curve out of sight. She was inside the girl again . . .

She put her foot hard down. She had been out long enough now. Lawrence would be getting anxious, and she should be standing cool and lovely at his side, introducing him to Mother's friends. She would wear her white crocheted dress which had a white satin ribbon for a waistband and long tight sleeves. But it left her neck bare and was wide at the shoulders. White again. It was amusing . . .

The trees were spinning past her now. She thought she must watch out for bends and change down in plenty of time as she had been taught. The first one she took beautifully, Lawrence would have been proud of her. Lawrence, she thought, soon, my love . . . She would begin now to look for a place to turn, she had been out far too long. It had been a senseless thing to do, Lawrence would not approve. A farm track or a gate. She began to take her eyes off the road from time to time. The next bend was still far ahead, she could see the smooth sunlit curve with something black in its centre, a shadow, perhaps.

A farm track or a gate. Here, coming fast towards her, was a gap on the left-hand side of the road. This would probably do. Immediately she thought, no, it won't, it's too soon. She was almost on the bend, she must have been travelling faster than she realised. Change down, change down! But her speed was too great and she had forgotten how to double de-clutch.

She was on it now. The car was straddling the black patch on the road which had an irridescent gleam. Not a shadow after all. The car slid away from her hands sideways across the road. She clutched the wheel again, trying to right it, but it seemed to have a will of its own. She tried again, hearing her own screams in her ears, seeing the row of trees . . .

'It's a shame to talk shop,' Lawrence said. His small talk had completely gone in his anxiety. Why didn't she appear? 'In your work I expect you've had to evolve some kind of credo for yourself. I should imagine you've to try to be a whole person so that you can help people who aren't. How, for instance, do you reconcile the sadness you must see with,' he found he was copying Susskind's gesture, the outspread hands, the shrug, so much for origins, 'a Merciful Being?'

'I don't go in for reconciliations, I don't think the human mind is equipped for that. I do what's nearest.' His dark eyes smiled at Lawrence. 'Lao-tse says that having completed a task means having become eternal.'

'Could you include our experiences in that, and perhaps our . . .' There was a hush in the room. Lawrence was not immediately aware of it because he was in that rarefied state which comes from high thinking judiciously blended with alcohol. But suddenly he heard his own voice loud in his ears and was embarrassed.

And then he saw her. Julia. She was standing at the door, dishevelled, her trousers were dirty, her face was tear-stained.

55

'Good gracious, Julia,' it was Lydia's cool voice, 'what have you been doing?'

The girl's eyes swung wildly about the room, ignoring her mother who had started towards her, Grant behind. Lawrence saw the pitiful face at the same moment as their eyes met. He was half across the room when she launched herself on him, pressing her body against his. She was shaking violently. 'I've crashed the car, Lawrence, it wasn't my fault, I've crashed the car! A man gave me a lift. It's ruined, Lawrence, crashed against a tree . . .' Her voice grew wilder. 'You tell them, Lawrence, you tell them.' She burst into a fit of weeping, putting her face against his shoulder. 'Lawrence . . .'

'Hush,' he said, 'hush, it's done now, it doesn't matter . . .' Looking over her head at the startled faces in the room, and especially at Lydia's, he realised that now he would have to marry her. They had seen her need. She needed him. He had to protect her. They made way for them, and he helped her, weeping, from the room.

6

They went by road to Sicily for their honeymoon because Julia said she was afraid to fly, and Lawrence in his love would have done anything to please her. In fact she was afraid to drive, but *her* love was greater than her fear. She still at times saw the shattered Triumph in her dreams.

To ease the driving they put the car on the train in Paris at the Gare de Charolais, and then had to hang around the gloomy station for hours before they were allowed to board the train. But nothing could affect her happiness. She sat in the waiting-room with her hand tucked in Lawrence's arm, and after a time they went

56

out to the bar and bought some sandwiches.

'Sandwiches!' Lawrence said, seeing what they were offered, 'a great hunk of crusty bread, no butter, a slice of mouldy meat roll!'

'You shouldn't complain about food in foreign countries,' she said, 'I learned that when I was in Vevey.'

'All right, my love. We'll have two brandies to wash it down.' He drank the brandy and munched away, his eyes on her.

'Don't,' she said, 'I know what you're thinking . . .'

When they went back to the waiting-room an old priest in a black cassock and wearing an unlikely topee was sitting where they had been. '*C'est ma place*,' he grumbled. His bare feet in their sandals were dirty and deformed with horny nails, once he got up and searched in the litter bin, returning with a discarded bag of sweets which he proceeded to eat, poking about in the bag with his nose an inch away from it.

'Where could he have come from?' Julia asked when at last it was time to go to the train. 'Such poverty, Lawrence. Did you see his poor feet? Those are the kind of feet that Jesus washed . . . Do you think he was going to sleep in that waiting-room?'

'Probably. Perhaps he wasn't a priest at all. Perhaps he stole the habit.'

'Oh, no, he had an honest face. But the sadness of it! Sometimes the sadness of other people almost breaks my heart.'

He was disturbed. 'You mustn't be so sensitive, darling.'

There had been a mistake in the booking and they had to share a sleeping compartment with two Frenchmen who looked like commercial travellers. He was sure Julia didn't sleep much. They were in the bottom berths, and in the middle of the night he stretched out his hand to her. He felt her put it against her face.

But at last it was morning and two pairs of trousered

57

legs were lowered from the top berths to be followed by
two correctly accoutred gentlemen even to brief-cases.
'*Bon jour, Madame, Monsieur,*' they said, with correct
French bows. In spite of the discomfort the train
journey had given them a good start, and they sped down
the Italian motorway from Milan, which, although it was
July, was not too crowded.

They stopped for their first night at Florence because
Julia had never been there. He thought the two-
dimensional landscape of Florence as he remembered it,
dark cypresses superimposed on the paler hills, would
attract her, but instead she talked more about the boy she
had spoken to in a coffee bar who had hitched from
America. He wore a jersey embroidered with the words,
'I love all mankind. It's the people I don't like.'
He had the lost face which he now recognised was a per-
quisite for Julia's attention.

But Florence, which was going to be a romantic setting for their first night together, provided a meal which
made Julia unromantically sick, and they were in the car
again the next morning and speeding southwards before
she began to recover. 'I'm so sorry, Lawrence, truly. It
wasn't intentional. And then we hadn't slept the night
before . . .'

And so they were in an unlikely motel in Naples before Lawrence made her his own. He teased her with the
words. He considered his forbearance had been admir-
able, but he had a secret fear that there might be
difficulties, he didn't quite know what. He was prepared
for tears, or some kind of transport, not necessarily of
delight, but instead she was passionate and pleasing. He
should have remembered the attic in Wimbledon. He
flagged before she did. The dawn had come before they
finally went to sleep in a tangle of bedclothes.

Seen in the daylight the motel which had been a welcome oasis the previous night was found to be in the
scrawniest part of the city. It had been fenced around

by white-painted wood, but when they took a short walk while the car was being serviced they saw that on the other side was another world, dark caves of houses with scrawny gardens and scrawnier hens scaping the dust, black old women pinning out black old underwear.

Julia held tightly to his arm. 'Why do people have to live in such misery? I can't bear to see it.' Her eyes were dark-stained and he loved her utterly. He bent and kissed her. 'You mustn't worry *for* people. How do you know they aren't happy? As you are happy. Aren't you?'

'Lawrence . . . happy.'

'Next stop Taormina.'

'I don't like this place. It spoils the thought of last night. When we were . . . you know, they were being poor and miserable in their hovels.'

'Nothing could spoil that,' he said, but in some subtle way it did alter last night, the luxury, the shining showers, the loving . . . nothing could spoil the loving, he thought. One imaginative one in the family was enough.

Julia loved the pool. It was oval except that on one side, to relieve the symmetry, she supposed, a U-shaped piece of paving jutted out into its blueness. At the far end of the oval there was a little bridge leading on to a stone platform with a glazed pottery pelican on it, a small gurgle coming from its raised beak. You could swim under the bridge but it was colder there out of the sun.

What she liked best to do was to try and capture the insects which landed on the pool, usually ladybirds. Lawrence found a hollow cane for her, and she padded about happily while he lay sunbathing, or more often, watching her. She knew that he had been worried about her after the accident. But that was all over now. She let Lawrence drive her up the corkscrew roads above Taormina until it seemed they were on a level with Etna. They roared downwards in the open car and she hadn't been too afraid. Nothing made her afraid as long as he

59

was there. If he left her for a short time it was like a shadow crossing the sun.

Once at night she tried to tell him of this. 'I can't live without you, Lawrence.'

He hesitated, then said smiling at her, 'Well, who's asking you to? Just tell me how you propose to get rid of me?'

She found interesting things for them to see. 'Don't let's go on those terrible organised tours. We'll find things for ourselves.' She was quicker than he was.

They would watch how the Sicilian peasants got up the steep steps which led from one street to another by hanging on to the tails of their burros. And were fascinated at the cleverness of the animal which halved the incline by walking from one end of the step to the other before it took a step upwards.

She found fishermen painting their boats on the beach, tremendous, fiddling work, Lawrence said. She liked the intricacy of the designs, like a knitting pattern. Once they had the luck to see a dancing horse pulling a painted cart at a fiesta.

'Lawrence, come and see, come and see!' She was daft with excitement. He left his wine to look with her, his arm round her waist.

'Look at its plumes, and its coat made of silver foil. And there's a band in the cart. Can you see?'

There was the smell of lemons everywhere and love in the afternoons. The wine was golden.

She loved the narrow streets, the Sicilians who pushed near her, 'The Mafia is after you,' Lawrence's grin when he said this, and the absent, dreamy look which meant that he would soon say, 'isn't it time for our siesta?'

On their last night they stood on the terrace with the town falling giddily away to the sea and the houses clinging like lizards to a wall. Occasionally there was a dull glow which was Etna erupting and which Lawrence said didn't mean much. It was a remote chance that there would be another Herculaneum.

A long time ago she had been high up on a haystack. Long, long ago . . . It was in the farm near Crawford's grandparents' house. She saw him standing far beneath her, his face white in the dry dusk of the barn. 'Jump, Julia. There's a great heap of hay here. It's as soft as soft. Jump . . . it's just like flying. I did it . . .'

'Lawrence,' she said, 'what would happen if I stood on this rail and held my arms out? Should I float down?'

'Try it.' He pretended to help her up but she fell into his arms and stood in their circle hearing the loud beating of his heart.

'I remember,' she said, 'long, long ago, how I jumped from a haystack . . . I honestly felt I was flying . . .'

'Who put you up to it?'

'My friend, Crawford North. He was always thinking up things, always thinking up things . . .' She felt her smile twist, closed her mind against what she was seeing.

Lawrence was teasing her, kissing her in between words, 'I want it . . . to be . . . clearly understood . . . that Crawford . . . North . . . is not allowed . . . in . . . on our honeymoon.' And then, more softly, 'There's only room in the bed for two.'

They crossed the Channel in the Hovercraft and it was as if the journey had been a catalyst. When they had been through the Customs and were in the car driving towards London she talked incessantly.

'Honestly, Lawrence, it's been absolutely perfect. Our honeymoon. Moonhoney . . . Blake says somewhere, "moony." Yes, it was about Beulah, that's it, Beulah, "a soft universe, feminine, lovely." Did you find me feminine and lovely, Lawrence? I absolutely loved you all the time. And Taormina. What did you think of Taormina? Steps, steps, steps, more steps, a Madonna with an Alice band of electric light bulbs, the Sicilian wine which must be the wine of paradise, Etna glowering, that's good, glowering, and, oh, the dancing horse! Shall we ever see anything so fine again as that dancing horse? Its serious face. Trying to do its best. What do you think of when you think of Taormina, Lawrence?'

'You, you and more you. Now keep quiet for a minute. I'll have to concentrate on this traffic. God, I had forgotten about this traffic, if anything is going to remind me that I'm coming home, this is it. It's ten times worse than when we went away.'

But when they had parked the car and she had started running up the stairs towards the flat, he had to admit that he was excited too. Honeymoons were all right, but coming back to one's own place was even better. Here they would be happy and grow like each other, and every day would be a new day because they were together.

'Kate Henderson asked me for the key,' he said. 'I hope you don't mind. She lives very near here, and she said she would like to put in a few things for us to eat, and to dust around a bit.'

'That was extremely kind of her. So thoughtful. But there was no need.' It was Lydia speaking, and he had to smile.

'I know there was no need, but Kate's that kind of girl, thoughtful. Here we are.' He put the key in the door and turned the lock. 'Do you want me to carry you over the threshold?'

'No,' she was gay, radiant, how lucky he was, 'I'm not a bit superstitious. Besides you would take too long. I'm dying to see my house.' She walked quickly down the long corridor and pushed open the door of the living-room.

Coming up behind her he saw that the place was fresh and polished. He even fancied that he smelled Kate's perfume, 'light with a kick' he had told her the night they went to Julia's dance. It seemed aeons away.

The table was set with golden-coloured mats, and there was a bottle of wine. The candles were white. On a side-table there was a white vase of flowers. 'Kate has been busy,' he said, 'I bet there's food in the frig too. Look at the flowers.'

'Yes, I see them,' she spoke slowly, 'white vase, white flowers. Lilies, aren't they?' She went over and touched them. 'Nice.' She stepped back and stood motionless, he wondered if she was still admiring them but her back seemed tense, her voice when she spoke still slow, 'White . . . a burning kind of white. I never thought you could have a burning white, like white fire.' Now the words were running into one another, 'And the shape of the vase. When I came into the room it was as if there was nothing else in it except that white vase. It burned itself on my brain so that everywhere I looked in the room I saw it, like when you look directly at the sun and then there are blinding little spots . . .'

'I think you're making a hell of a lot of fuss about the vase, Julia. It's very nice, but that's all.'

'You don't see its . . . its *significance*?'

'No.' A creeping feeling of unease invaded him, like a cold draught in a hot room, like vague toothache, like the beginning of a headache. 'You're a funny girl,' he held out his arms and she came into them, 'my own funny girl.'

'For better or for worse?'

Or for worse. He hadn't said the words.

'Hold me tightly, Lawrence, tightly, tightly.'

She could always arouse him, the unease slipped away to be replaced by strong desire, making his body harden. 'Julia,' he said, 'you drive me mad.' His hands were under her jersey, she was heavy on him, he could scarcely speak as if his throat had constricted to a narrow tube. 'It's either bed or my dinner on the table in five minutes,' he said, trying to laugh.

'I'm not hungry,' she said, 'and what's wrong with

63

that?' She pointed to a soft Mongolian hearthrug at the fireplace, a wedding present from someone.

'It's damnable,' he said, 'we've been married for two whole weeks and I'm like a lovesick fool when you come near me.'

'Who's complaining?' Her voice was muffled. She was pulling her jersey over her head.

7

They settled into a comfortable pattern of living, one which was not greatly removed from their single state. In the morning Lawrence set off for the office and didn't return until six o'clock. He thought it was a long day for Julia to be alone, but she assured him she didn't mind in the least. He thought this was probably true.

She was in love with the flat, with the idea of having a house of her own. She enjoyed shopping, she could spend hours poking about in the back streets for unusual bits of junk, not the mass-produced commodities of the big stores. In the afternoon she went up to her workroom, and sometimes she was there when he came home at night and he had to disturb her. Once he found her sitting before a mass of drawings which must have taken hours, her hands untouched by clay.

She jumped up as if covered with guilt. 'Oh, Lawrence! I've wasted my time. The day's flown! Mother came in the morning,' (Lydia was a frequent dropper-in), 'and she wanted to go out for lunch. And then we trailed round the shops, not the ones I like, the big opulent ones where the people have hard faces. She's always matching something, she's got eternal little swatches of material in her bag for curtains or cushions or carpets or dresses. She can't carry colours in her head, she says. I can. Do you remember the Sicilian carts? I couldn't work when she went away. I've been amusing myself.' She showed him a gouache of a Sicilian cart with the childish colours in their precise patterns.

Once when he was reading some stuff he had brought home with him she disappeared around midnight and he thought she had gone to bed. When he went into the kitchen for a drink of water he found her on her knees scrubbing the floor.

'Julia!' He was horrified. 'I thought you had Mrs. Thing for that.'

'No, she's stopped coming.' She tucked a loop of hair over her ear. 'She has a sick little boy and I told her she mustn't come back until he was quite better. Can you imagine that little boy sitting up in bed, feeling so absolutely ill and waiting for his mother to come back to him? You need company when you're ill. Remember how I needed you at Florence?'

'To hold your head!' He laughed at her. 'Aren't you tired?'

'Tired?' She splashed a sopping cloth on the floor and started to scrub vigorously. 'Tired! I've got so much energy that I can't use it all up.'

'Well, come to bed,' he said sensibly enough.

In bed he found it was true.

And yet some mornings she didn't get up, lying with her face turned away from him. He knew that her periods were irregular and that she suffered pain. He would tenderly gather the clothes around her and bring her a cup of tea. 'Julia, Julia, darling.' Her hand would come out to him as she lay on her face. She needed him. He found it infinitely touching.

'I think we must ask Kate to dinner one night,' he said, when they had been home for a few weeks. Autumn had come now. Dinners were better by candlelight.

'Yes, we must.'

'I see her in the office, of course, and I'm beginning

to feel guilty about it. She went on holiday directly after we came home so it didn't matter. But she was very kind getting things ready for us when we came back.'

'Yes, the flowers . . .'

'Did you ring her? You said you were going to.'

'Yes, I did. But she was busy, and I wrote a formal little note of thanks. Mother says it's still correct to write the formal little note.' He had to smile.

'I thought we might ask her with Richard Lewis. He's a doctor and a great friend of hers. I'd like him to take you on. Unless you have a doctor in Wimbledon you'd rather keep.'

'No, I didn't like him. He was the fashionable kind. You could only see him by appointment. How can you know in advance that you're going to be ill?'

'Well, will you ring Kate?'

'Shall you see her today?'

'Yes, I think so.'

'Well, *you* ask her.'

'It's more correct for the hostess to do that.' Then, seeing her woebegone face he laughed and kissed her, 'All right.' He was amused to think that her reluctance might be rooted in jealousy.

He ran into her father in the men's washroom. 'Hello, there,' Grant said, tugging at the roller towel, 'behold the bridegroom cometh. I've kept away to give you time to settle down, although I don't think Lydia has. But I said no State Visits for a time.'

'You know you're always welcome.'

'Thanks. You're both happy?'

'Yes, very happy. It's ridiculous,' he laughed, 'excuse the fatuous expression I'm wearing. She's a star turn, our Julia.'

'Yours now,' Grant smiled.

'I never know what she's going to be up to next. Quite unpredictable. And she's so happy on her own. Sometimes I get worried about that.'

'She's always been the same. I know it worried Lydia a lot, but we are as we are. It's no good pushing people.'

'No, I see that. Anyhow, she's not anti-social. I've to ask Kate Henderson and a friend to dinner this week. Kate was very kind and set the house in order. A lot of the stuff had still to be unwrapped.'

'Lydia had offered but Julia said no.'

'Oh . . . perhaps I've put my foot in it. But Kate, well, she's Kate. No one could dislike her.'

'She's got a large heart. And a clever mind. By the way, talking shop, she sold a serial in Amsterdam not so long ago and now there's been some trouble with the copyright so she's having to make another trip. I don't quite know when. I think this is where the firm should come down heavily with a show of top brass. Would you care to go over and make important noises?'

'Do you think it's necessary?' He immediately thought of telling Julia he was going, and her reaction. They hadn't been parted as yet, but then again she was self-sufficient, wasn't she? No girl would spend so much time on her own if she weren't self-sufficient, and for that matter she could stay at Wimbledon for the night.

'Yes, I think it would be best. It's an important contract and the Dutch agent has been angling for this firm for a long time. You needn't say too much to Julia about it.' Grant's face was bland. Was it a delicate hint not to mention Kate?

He went along to Kate's room before he started to work. She had her hair cut a new way, he noticed, short and off her face, but whorled on the top. 'It suits you.' He flicked at one of the whorls with his finger.

'You're a married man now,' she said, 'that's out.'

'Can I prevent my natural tendencies when I see a pretty girl?'

'Natural tendencies are out too. They become unnatural when you're married.' She smiled at him. 'How's Julia?'

67

'Oh, fine. She's suggested that you come and have dinner with us some night this week. Bring Richard Lewis. That is, if you're still seeing him?'

'Richard is one of my built-in conveniences.'

'Why don't you marry him? You'd make a great doctor's wife.'

'You're a come-on-in-the-water's-fine type now. Changed days. I'm not ready for marriage.' She spoke shortly. 'Did Julia mention a special evening?'

'No, we leave it to you.'

'Shall we say Thursday? That's Richard's night off. You don't want him being blamed for the soufflé collapsing if he's got to go out in the middle of it.'

'Okay, we'll say Thursday, and just in case I'll ask Julia to make a non-collapsible soufflé. That's the domestic issue settled. This trouble you're having in Amsterdam, Kate. I've read the correspondence. They're in the wrong, you know. There's no copyright protection for plots.'

'That's what I told them. But I sometimes think the Dutch don't believe in the emancipation of women. I find them looking *at* me instead of listening *to* me. There's a subtle difference.'

'You're too pretty. Grant suggests that I fly over and sort them out.'

'That's what's needed. I've made the appointment for, let me see,' she flicked over the appointments diary which lay on her desk, 'Monday, 6th September, ten-thirty. I intend to go over on Sunday evening . . . I don't suppose there's any need for us to go at the same time.'

'I don't agree. I think a concerted front is indicated . . .' He hesitated.

'Would Julia mind if you did?'

He raised his eyebrows in pretended astonishment. 'Mind! Not a bit of it.' Well, most husbands had to be diplomatic from time to time. He needn't mention that Kate would be going too. He thought of saying, 'Don't mention it to Julia,' and then couldn't bring himself to do so. Or of taking her with him. But this was a test case, he told himself. He must at least give the impression of being master in his own house. 'We'll fix up the details later. Well, Thursday evening for you and Richard? Julia will be delighted.'

She said she was, absolutely delighted, and there began a complete cleaning campaign of the flat which exhausted her, so that for the first time she turned away from him in bed. Her body felt light and boneless under his hand. She took it out of herself, he thought tenderly, punished herself all the time. What would she be like with a couple of kids?

They had never talked about a family. He thought for the first time that perhaps she was enough to contend with at the moment, and dismissed that as disloyal.

In the morning she was fresh-eyed and happy. 'I had a marvellous sleep. Well, I'm straight now. All the cleaning done. Everything spick and span.'

'You don't think Richard and Kate are going to go around looking under beds and in cupboards?'

'It's *knowing* it's clean that counts. Today I'll plan the menu and buy in the food. I've phoned Mother and said I'll be very busy. She's popping in a little too often.'

'She's glad to see you a happy girl.'

'She's glad to see me a married woman. She wants to have married women's secrets, confidences, I don't like her to pry.'

'I'm sure she's only trying to be helpful.'

'People say that when all the time they're curious.'

He couldn't fault anything when he came home on Thursday evening. The table was set, the candles were ready to light, Julia was in a trouser suit which outdid anything of Kate's.

'I bought this today,' she said, whirling round for his inspection, 'I remembered what you said about Mother

69

and asked her to go with me. She was delighted.'

'Because you made her feel wanted.' He kissed her. 'I like your mandarin collar. Only girls with slender necks should wear them.'

Kate, as if she had known about the trouser suit, was in a long dress. Whereas Julia had become boyish, Kate was now womanly. And she was good with Julia. 'Seeing you in that I hereby vow I'll never wear a trouser suit again. You spoil it for everyone else, you hipless wonder.'

It was good to talk to Richard. 'You're putting on weight, Lawrence,' he accused him laughingly.

'I know what you're thinking and it's true!'

They moved together to the drinks table. Julia had taken Kate into their bedroom. 'Julia looks ravishing,' Richard said. 'There are looks and looks. Kate has the comforting sort but one blinks when one meets Julia again. Aren't you afraid to take her out? You'd think there was an electric bulb, a two-fifty watt, inside her.'

'Yes, she's got a tremendous capacity for being . . .' he hesitated, looking for the right word, 'joyful.'

'And therefore an equal capacity for being the opposite?'

'I haven't noticed that much. Sometimes in the mornings . . . but most of the time she's happy.'

'I wish I could follow your example.'

'Kate?'

'Yes, there's no one else for me. Never has been. I thought when you were hitched it would be plain sailing.'

'What do you mean?'

'Come off it. You must have been blind . . .'

Julia's voice interrupted him. The girls were in the room again. 'A drink for Kate, Lawrence. I'm going to disappear into the kitchen if you don't mind. I'm only practising to be a cool hostess yet.' She laughed, looked shy, stood awkwardly for a moment and then said, 'Well, if you'll excuse me . . .' and went out. Lawrence smiled. 'You're our first dinner guests.'

'We're highly honoured,' Richard said. 'She's engaging, isn't she, almost like a child.'

Not in bed, Lawrence wanted to say, not in bed. He turned to Kate. 'I know what you want. Whisky and soda, isn't it?'

'How did you guess?'

'Don't forget I knew you first.' Their eyes met when he handed her the glass. Surely she hadn't been, well, gone on him, as Richard suggested? He remembered the night in her flat before they went to Julia's dance and thought that he had been misleading.

After a time Julia came back looking important and said, 'Would you sit down at the table now, please.' They had no dining room.

Lawrence got up and pulled out a chair for Kate, standing behind it. 'Come on, Kate. I can tell you . . . yes, you sit there, Richard . . . I can tell you this dinner is either going to be a bloody marvel or a complete disaster. I'm as much in the dark as you are.'

As it happened it was almost perfect. The hors-d'œuvres were exceptionally *variées*, the Bœuf Stroganoff was creamy and succulent, she didn't spoil the meal by heavy sweets at the end but served a fresh fruit salad. She had gone to trouble with the cheese. The praise from Kate and Richard was lavish.

'You mustn't lay it on so thick,' he said, as he refilled their glasses, 'she's likely to dance a fandango any minute. She thrives on praise.'

'Well, I hear she's a very clever girl.' Kate smiled at Julia. 'While we're doing our mundane tasks Julia is being creative. I can believe it after this meal. I hear you sculpt as well.'

'Sculpt is too grand. I model in clay. Very badly.'

'Could we see some of it afterwards?' Richard asked. 'Well . . .'

'*I'm* proud of her. *I'll* show you,' Lawrence said.

'Don't you find it lonely?' Kate asked. 'I seem to work

71

best with the clatter of typewriters in the background.'

'No, not at all. I don't like noise. And then I've so much to do that it would waste time to have to talk to people.' Her speech became faster. 'I'm doing a series of children's heads completely from imagination. I want to do a perfect child, *the* perfect child, and then I'll change it as it grows up, a new one for every phase . . . and as well I'm doing a lot of reading, serious reading.'

'You hadn't told me this, Julia,' Lawrence said.

'I don't tell you everything. You see,' she looked round the table, 'I feel terribly at a disadvantage with all you clever people who go out into the world every day. So I've got to self-educate myself. I don't know quite what I'm trying to find, truth, perhaps. Everything that happens seems so chaotic, things press in on you. I feel that if I found the key somewhere everything would make sense, no, more than that, a pattern, *mean* something, a pattern of meaning. Don't you ever feel this?'

'Every morning when I see my desk,' Kate said.

'And think of the joy when you found it! There you would be, right in the centre and understanding it, no, that's too shallow, completely involved, *it*, like the sun rather than the sun's rays, like the centre of a storm . . . like the eye of a daisy. Sometimes you feel you're on the point of it, when you read something. Yesterday there was this poem, "Little Lamb who made thee?" *Who* made thee? You see, everyone's asking. Everyone absolutely is asking. Sometimes little things seem to be on the point of telling you, a vase of flowers, a chair at a window . . .'

Richard spoke. His eyes were on Julia. 'I think Lawrence is extremely lucky. A girl who thinks as well as being beautiful.'

'You're teasing me.'

'On the contrary. Could we see your heads?'

'You mean now?'

'I don't think I could eat a morsel more and Kate daren't.'

'Lead on,' Lawrence said. 'I'll make the coffee while you're showing off, darling.'

He was glad to move, to occupy himself in the kitchen measuring out the precise spoonfuls of coffee, he saw there were numerous notes on the blackboard he had put up for her as a giant memorandum pad, and he read them idly while he stood by the percolator.

'Four *heaped* tablespoonfuls of coffee to three pints of water.' Then came lengthy instructions for the Bœuf Stroganoff, the preparation of the hors-d'œuvres, even a diagram of the table with their names written in squares which no doubt represented chairs. 'Kate.' 'Me.' 'Richard.' And then in the remaining square he noticed that his own name was written over something else. He peered and detected a capital C, quite clearly.

For God's sake, I've been sleeping with the woman for more than two months now. She surely knows my name . . . his heart knocked irregularly on his ribs. Once. His face went cold. 'Crawford.' He said it out loud. And then he laughed at himself. You're like a pregnant woman, full of whimsies.

When Kate and Richard came downstairs they were singing Julia's praises. Kate said, 'This girl's a perfectionist, Lawrence. She should sell some of those heads. The latest one is beautiful, really beautiful.'

'It's not for sale,' Julia said, she had sat down at the low table to pour the coffee, 'it's for Lawrence.'

'Is it, darling?' he asked, 'you never told me.'

'Didn't I? But you know that everything I do is for you.'

There was a little pause. Lawrence handed the cups around. Kate said, 'Thank you.' Her eyes were clear, no loaded look. 'If this coffee Lawrence has made is as good as your dinner, Julia, well, I suggest that you start a restaurant and Richard and I will come every evening and dine on the house.'

'You're very kind.' He saw Julia's eyes as she looked at Kate. They were full of trust. Thank God that she likes her, he thought, I hope they become good friends.

'By the way, Richard,' he said, after they had chatted for a time, 'I always meant to tell you this. Before Julia and I were married I was down at their place in Dorset for the weekend and met your former chief, Dr. Susskind.'

'Did you? That's interesting.'

'There's a further tie-up. Gerry might be doing a translating job for me.'

'Good. What did you think of him, I mean, Leo?'

'Extremely approachable, I found. We had quite a deep conversation, for me, that is, probably nothing to him.'

'I'm going down next weekend, as a matter of fact. It's my monthly one off, and since Kate is leaving me and flying off to Amsterdam with you it's better than staying in London.' There was an imperceptible pause and then his face went a deep turkey red.

Kate spoke quickly, but he thought she looked shaken, 'Those boring trips! Half the office being sent by Grant just because of trouble with a measly old serial. Julia,' she smiled, 'I was wondering if you would like to meet me for lunch some day?'

'That's very thoughtful of you. I should be delighted.' Julia's face was expressionless. She got up. 'I'll go and make more coffee.' She was gone for a long time, and Lawrence heard the rattle of dishes from the kitchen.

'Is she washing up?' Kate whispered. 'Shall I go and help?'

'No, don't.' He didn't know why he said that. 'She goes at things at a hell of a lick. Just leave her to do it.'

'Did I put my foot in it?' Richard looked miserable.

'No, I'm the one.' Kate turned to Lawrence. 'I'm

74

sorry, I mean, about blabbing to Richard. It was unforgivable but unintentional. It was just that Richard asked me out and I gave him my real reason without thinking.'

'Think no more of it.'

There was a pause. Kate said, 'We must go fairly soon. I'm sure Julia must be tired.'

'There's no hurry.' He was casual, when all he wanted to do was to shut the door behind them.

He had imagined that she would say something about Amsterdam when Kate and Richard had gone. He tried to give her an opportunity. 'Did you like them, Julia?'

'Oh, yes, very much. They're kind all the way through. I don't think it's a pretence.'

'I should take Kate up on that lunch date when she phones you. You can do with a girl friend.'

'I had them.' She looked tired and pale.

'Yes, but you've lost touch now. Take her up on it. She'll probably marry Richard and then I imagine we might become quite close.' He felt a little bleakness as he said that, was it a vestigial tail of jealousy? Well, Kate was special. He had never been in love with her, of course, but she was, well, rather special . . .

He took the plunge. 'That Amsterdam thing, Julia.'

'What Amsterdam thing?' They were now in their bedroom and she was undressing with her back to him.

'I've been asked by your father to go over and straighten out a client. Nothing to do with Kate at all.'

'But she's going too.'

'Yes. She's in charge of foreign sales. But I shall probably not see her.'

She put her nightdress over her head and then turned to him. 'But I think you should, Lawrence. After all, they're going to be our best friends. It wouldn't be polite not to.'

'Well, it isn't important anyhow. Only *you* are.' He came towards her and put his arms round her. Her long

75

light body was against his and he noticed again the incredible slenderness. Richard would have said definitely not the child-bearing type, too narrow.

He ran his hand slowly down her spine. Why did he think that? Did he already want to procreate himself, like all men in their sexual egotism? But only when she was ready. She would settle down in a year or two, and then there would be babies and she wouldn't have enough time to spend in her workroom and she would grow a little fatter and a little more comfortable . . . He thought that he should not have reservations like this.

'Darling, what is this special thing you're doing for me upstairs?'

'It isn't ready,' he felt her body stiffen, 'it absolutely isn't ready . . .'

'Okay, okay,' he said, 'come to bed.'

There wasn't any need for reservations here. She was abandoned, erotic, she moaned in his arms. Her beauty was in her body too in the shape and the feel and the rightness of it. A fine body was a dispensation from heaven. He was drained physically and mentally when at last they went to sleep.

I forgot to compliment her on the evening, he thought, the cooking and all the trouble she went to, the trouser suit. Even her diagram on the board . . . he pushed that one away. 'C'. Someone's name beginning with 'C', rapidly rubbed out, a slip of the chalk. Don't say it. Don't even think it.

And he must tell her in a husbandly tone that it was bad form to go and rattle dishes when your guests were still there. It made them feel unwanted.

Oh, Julia . . . he thought, and fell abruptly into sleep.

Sometime during the night he felt her body against his, and heard a choking noise. She couldn't be weeping, could she, after such a happy night.

8

The next week they had another dinner party. Lydia and Grant this time. Lawrence was amused to find that the menu was the same as that which they had for Kate and Richard, but that Julia had discarded her trouser suit for a long dress rather like the one Kate had worn.

She had told him that they had lunched together. That Kate had asked her to call at the office and had introduced her to Janet Mearns, her secretary, because Janet was an amateur painter. 'Water colours,' she said to Lawrence, 'cottages with roses round the door.' He didn't often hear her being snide.

'And I met your secretary too.'

'Maggie? What did you think of Maggie?'

'Well, she's odd. She started to type halfway through our conversation, banging her machine like mad.'

'That's because she's prickly and probably couldn't bear to look at you. You're ravishing, you know, darling, and Maggie is past her prime.' He thought as he spoke that this girl, his dear wife, was absolutely without vanity.

'Is she in love with you?'

'She used to be,' he said to tease her, 'but once she got to know me she changed her mind.'

She didn't smile. Her look was considering. 'We went afterwards to a boutique called "Step Right In".'

'Ridiculous name.'

'It was to please Kate. Girls go to boutiques together. I got this dress there. They both said it was just me. Is it just me, Lawrence?'

'It's only just you when you've no clothes on.'

'The owner, Joanne, Kate said she's called, gave it to me at a special price because she said it was good to see someone who could really wear it after watching fat girls struggling into two sizes too small for them. She said if I ever wanted to model clothes she'd take me on. A salesgirl cum model, she said. But I absolutely couldn't ever want to sell clothes or walk up and down wearing them. It would be such a waste of time. Today was a waste of time.'

'It's a change for you.'

'I like my workroom better.'

'As long as you're happy. Perhaps later on we'll have a family.' He chanced his arm.

'Perhaps . . .' she hadn't said anything more.

During dinner they all seemed to be on their best behaviour. Lydia was beautifully turned-out as usual, and made polite conversation, praising the flat, Julia's cooking, asking Lawrence about his work.

Julia was coolly efficient, an inflection from Lydia's voice seemed to creep into her own, her remarks were conventional as if she had picked up Lydia's way of talking on the surface without revealing any of her own personality.

'Lawrence is going to Amsterdam next weekend,' she said when they were having coffee, 'it's good for the firm's image.'

Lawrence looked across at Grant and caught his eye. He looked faintly surprised, and one eyebrow was raised as he took a sip of coffee. 'That's how I like to hear a daughter of mine speaking,' he said, 'the interests of the firm at heart.'

'Come home for that weekend, darling,' Lydia said, 'don't I know those frequent trips all over the place! I've always said one must make a life for oneself.'

'Yes,' Julia's face was serene, 'one must absolutely make a life for oneself.'

'We've got a very good bridge club going now,' Lydia produced one of the thin brown cigars she permitted herself after dinner, 'you don't mind, darling?' waving it, 'there are quite a few young wives in it . . .' Her voice trailed away as she looked at Julia.

'It's no good, Mother. You know that.'

'Well won't you come home in any case? I could ask some of the friends who were at the wedding, the Gardiners and the Wards are always asking about you. Some young brides make a point of keeping in touch with girls of their own age . . . Judy Ward, I mean, Thomson, is home by the way.'

'Why?'

'Well . . . her husband has left her. After using up all her money, I may say. The Wards have been most generous. No blame could be laid at *their* door.' She tapped the cigar in the ashtray, delicately. 'So would you like to come home for the weekend?'

'It isn't a weekend, Lydia,' Lawrence interrupted, 'I go on Sunday evening simply so that I shall be there for a Monday morning appointment, but, of course, it would be nice for Julia to go home if she wants to.'

'Julia?' Lydia pursued.

'No, thanks, Mother. I've got absolutely so much to do. There's . . . shopping, and . . . and . . .' she looked around the room, 'oh, yes, I've got to get new curtains for here.'

'But you've just got new ones! And I don't think it would be wise to spend too much money here. After all, you ought to be looking for a house, nice as this flat is.'

'I'm putting these up in our bedroom. The colour jumps at you.'

'They seem very quiet to me. And in any case they'll jump, as you put it, wherever they are.' Lydia looked at the fairly discreet kingfisher blue curtains.

'We don't have our light on much there,' Lawrence grinned at Lydia.

'I'm extremely sensitive to colour.' Julia looked hounded, and he wanted to get up and put an arm round her, leave my Julia . . . 'That trouser suit we bought, Mother. I don't think I'll wear it again.'

'But scarlet on a fair girl like you is dramatic. So right! The assistant agreed with me.'

79

'I don't really want to be dramatic . . . I must, I must
. . .' She got up. 'I'll bring you a larger ashtray, that one's
no good . . .'

Lawrence turned to Grant. 'Come over here and leave
them to it.' They reseated themselves on a sofa at the
far end of the room.

Grant said softly, 'Lydia will have to stop pushing her
around now that she's married.'

'I think Julia knows what she wants.' But he felt uneasy and changed the subject. 'By the way, Grant, I've
wanted to chat to you about the Parmentier business.'

'There's no rush. We won't be publishing until next
year. Costs are getting prohibitive.'

'I'm waiting for some chapters from Gerry Susskind.'

'For comparison?'

'Yes. I remember years ago my father reproaching my
mother for getting several estimates for decorating the
house and holding up the job, and she said, "How else
would I find out which one is the cheapest?" '

'Where did your parents live?'

'Cheltenham. They died within a year of each other.
My father had cancer and my mother a coronary, the
reverse of the usual.'

'Sad. Isn't that Kate Henderson's home town?'

'Yes.'

He lowered his voice. 'Have you told Julia that Kate's
going to Amsterdam too?'

'Yes, she knows.' He kept quiet about Richard Lewis.
'She and Kate are quite thick now. Julia likes her. I think
Kate's trying hard to be friendly.'

'I'm sure that's genuine enough.' He sighed. 'You'd
think that a girl like Julia, brought up in the lap of
luxury, would have more friends than she knows what
to do with. Take yourself. I imagine you've got plenty?'

'Yes, plenty.' He remembered the bachelor parties before he met Julia, the gay times he had had, doing the
correct and the fun things, Ascot, discotheques, 'Oh, yes,

I had a whale of a time.' He hoped there was no regret in his voice.

'Haven't you seen any of them since you've been married?'

'Well, no, it changes things, you know that. They've been on the blower from time to time, and I have the odd business lunch with them, but Julia, well, I don't want to overload her with entertaining right away . . . You know, it, life, takes a lot out of her.'

'She overspends herself.' Their eyes met. Grant's were kind, discreet, nothing more. It's over to you, chum, now.'

Lawrence spoke after a pause. 'Well, we've drifted away from Parmentier's book. I want the translation to be good. It's a courtly love theme, a *Roman de la Rose* in modern dress. He's got a delicate touch, *nostalgie, Les Grandes Meulnes*, Remembrance of Things Past, you know what I mean . . . Susskind wants to meet Parmentier, that is, if we decide on him.'

'Yes, well, play it your own way, Lawrence, you'll let the unlucky one down lightly.' He laughed, looked, for an instant, shy, and Lawrence saw the fleeting resemblance between Julia and her father. 'I can't tell you, old chap, how glad I am that Julia's got you. You're strong enough for two, but gentle . . . I'm getting maudlin. She adores you and I think you're good for her. Maybe in a few years' time we'll hear the patter of childish voices, eh?'

'Feet,' Lawrence smiled, 'you *are* getting maudlin.' But he felt a bleakness, and at the same time an intense desire for a son, or a daughter, lovely like Julia, but . . . but, more ordinary . . . He laughed. 'Don't rush me. We've got a lot of living it up to do first.'

Lawrence was in the bedroom, packing his overnight bag. Julia stood beside him. She had come in, saying that she would look out his pyjamas and socks and handkerchiefs, but instead she had stood at the bed watching him as he went back and forth between the open drawers and his bag.

He looked up at her, 'You won't be lonely, will you, darling? I'll ring you if you like when I arrive in Amsterdam. I'll be there about six o'clock.'

'No, there's no need. I'll be perfectly all right. It's only for one night. Mother says this happens often.'

'Well, you would marry a tycoon.' She didn't laugh. 'Have you got to know anyone in the flats? There's a young boy downstairs. The right-hand door. He brought up our newspaper the other morning when you were in bed. It had gone to him by mistake. "I'm most awfully sorry to disturb you at this unearthly hour in the morning," he said. Very polite. Very queer.' Lawrence thought he was pretty safe mentioning him.

'Yes, he's nice. He types all day. I've heard the noise of the machine when it's quiet in the afternoons, but he has a boy friend who comes most lunch-times. I hear them laughing together. They seem to be very happy.'

'Well, don't hesitate to knock on his door if you're afraid about anything. Not that I think you will be for a moment,' he added quickly. 'I'll be back before you've time to realise it.'

'Lawrence, before you go, would you like to come up to the workroom and I'll show you my latest head? Have you time?'

'Of course I've time. Lead on.' He hadn't a great deal, and strangely enough he seldom went up to the attic. He couldn't explain why.

When he opened the door he saw the chaos, the open bin of clay, now he remembered the trouble they had had getting it up the narrow staircase. Why hadn't she taken up embroidery, or bird-watching, something nice and clean?

'Come in, don't be afraid.' Now, why should she say that?

He was surrounded by heads, mostly unfinished, some where even the features hadn't emerged, some where a too painstaking attention to detail took the life away from them. She took a cloth off one which was on the turntable, and he had an immediate impact of beauty like a smack on the face.

She was explaining patiently. 'I've tried so many. This one's the best, I think. That one,' she pointed across the room, 'I thought was all right until I discovered that the ears were too flat. Children's ears as a rule aren't tidy. They tend to stick out. I couldn't think where I could see a lot of children and then I remembered the dancing class round the corner. I had seen them being taken there by their mothers.'

'You didn't *go* there?'

'Yes. I asked the owner, Madame Montefiori, she's called, if I could just sit and watch. She looked a bit doubtful, but she said yes. I went every afternoon till I got it right.'

He was amazed. He didn't know her. She had been going in the afternoons to a children's dancing class, sitting watching them, and she hadn't told him. 'You never told me,' he said.

'No.' She pointed to another head, 'That one's chin should have been smaller. I had checked on all the obvious things and still couldn't see where I was wrong. And then one day I saw a very tiny boy at the class and I realised what I wasn't getting right.' She swivelled the turntable so that the head should face Lawrence.

'See.' She put her hand on the forehead. 'It's this, this bump.' Her thumb swept down. 'You see, you sweep in with the clay like this, and then the eyes are deepset in the skull. That's the bit that fills out as they grow older. I thought, now that I've got this one right I would do another one, and then another one, each one a little older, a little different...'

Lawrence looked at the head. There was a grizzle of

83

curls close to the skull, then the frontal protrusion she had spoken about. He traced it tenderly with his thumb as she had done, into the eye sockets, out again over the nose, down to the short upper lip, over the mouth, curved round to the small, indented chin. The whole thing had a touching appeal and he found himself moved almost to tears. There was something behind it all which he could only dimly grasp.

'It's for you, Lawrence,' she said, 'I give it to you.'

He took her in his arms. 'I can't take it, silly.' He found he had to blink, clear his throat.

'No, it's yours. I made it for you.'

When he was sitting in the plane beside Kate he thought again of the intensity of her blue eyes, the overall sadness of her face. Why should she be sad? She was loved, beautiful. He felt that it was an unconquerable sadness, something which all the loving in the world wouldn't dispel. 'No, it's for you,' she had said, 'I give it to you.'

9

After Lawrence had left, Julia went back to her workroom. She wouldn't make a meal yet, she thought, she didn't feel hungry. She lifted the cloth from the child's head, looked at the clay model, let the cloth fall back again. For the moment it was right. If she freed her mind, like putting a car out of gear, she would see flaws. That kind of looking always revealed flaws.

Lawrence had liked it. He had been touched. She had seen the tears start in his eyes and wanted to enclose him in her arms. But Lawrence never came to her for comfort. He was the strong one. He would have been embarrassed, or would he? 'Lawrence, my little boy,' she might say to him sometime, and gather him close in her arms.

She sat down at the littered table and saw the poem which she had been copying. It was good to have something disciplined to do at the same time as she was modelling. She needed something to retreat to when she was worried about the clay. She had thought to make this poem like an illuminated manuscript, it was to be in a bower of enamelled flowers with animals and birds.

This is what monks used to do, she thought, hour after sunny hour in shady cloisters, patiently inscribing. She had reached the second verse now. She began to colour the letters carefully, using a fine brush. This was the only thing water-colours were good for, in spite of 'The Fighting Temeraire' or the tomato-sauce sunsets. 'You're hard, hard, hard,' she said aloud, 'people think you're soft, soft, soft, but there's a hard core.'

Do you remember how you laughed when Lawrence told you of the man who had fallen in front of the train in the Tube? He had looked at you . . . but it wasn't laughter, it was a caught sob, or if it had been a laugh it was a laugh of horror. She heard the rushing of the train, the loud shriek of brakes, too late, too late . . .

'. . . Gave thee clothing of delight
Softest clothing, woolly bright
Gave thee such a tender voice
Making all the vales rejoice
Little Lamb who made thee
Dost thou know who made thee?'

Who? Who? Who . . . ?

The room was quiet, there wasn't even the London hum of noise because this was Sunday, quiet Sunday. Now she would find that pot of gold paint. If it was an illuminated manuscript it had to be illuminated. Perhaps if she did this really well they could have it framed and hang it in the bedroom like a sampler. 'East West Home's Best.'

Lawrence didn't like pictures on the bedroom wall. He absolutely didn't like pictures. Some people had mirrors, he told her. He would be teasing, of course, large mirrors, he said, hung above the bed. He liked to tease her, to make her laugh. Sometimes she felt she disappointed him, that her sense of humour wasn't very good.

She looked at her watch. Eight o'clock. Dinner time. She didn't like the thought of eating dinner alone. Without Lawrence the flat was desolate, peopled only with the children's heads and Julia.

What was it he had said? The boy in the flat downstairs, 'very polite, very queer,' and laughed when he said 'queer.' Well, there was no joke there surely. It wasn't funny. She would ask him if he would like to come up, and if his friend was there, he could come too. Everybody liked to be with their friend. Lawrence, you are my friend. And my lover. Just for coffee or a drink. She wouldn't keep them long but it would be nice company. Mrs. Leighton, Mother's help, used to say that, 'nice company.'

When she had made the coffee she went down the half flight of stairs and knocked on the door. 'Mr. Raymond Mills', it said on the neat little card. She had seen him once or twice when he was taking in his dustbin (really a plastic bag), which the tenants had to put out each morning for the janitor, Mr. Clewes. He had been most polite. Lawrence had noticed that too.

He opened the door. He was nice, he wore a mauve shirt and purple velvet trousers and he was smiling.

'Hello,' she said, 'I'm Julia, I live up there.' She half-turned and pointed.

'I know, dear,' he said, 'I've seen you when we've been working our fingers to the bone.'

'The dustbins?'

86

'That's right.'

'I've just made some coffee and I wondered if you would like to come up and have some, or a drink. Men often prefer a drink.'

'Well . . .' He had a nose that went straight into his forehead, she had always wanted to do a nose like that. Perhaps if they got to know each other really well she could ask him. 'Well, it's very sweet of you but I'm busy with my friend.'

'Would he like to come too? I've got plenty of coffee. Or drinks.'

'I'll ask him,' he said. He raised his voice. 'Come here a minute, Roger.'

Roger appeared. She thought he was handsome and she absolutely liked his eyes. Gazing eyes, not the kind which skimmed over you with a flat hard stare, like the lady shoppers.

'Hello,' she said, 'I just wondered if you would like some coffee since it's Sunday evening. I always think Sunday is the worst day of the week. And my husband has gone to Amsterdam which makes it even worse.'

'I like Sunday,' Raymond said, 'Roger always visits.'

'It says Mr. Raymond Mills on your card. Shall I call you Mr. Mills?'

'No, I prefer Raymond.' Roger giggled, 'So do I,' he said.

'Call me Raymond,' Raymond said, not looking at Roger but giggling too.

'Call me a taxi.' Roger was almost having hysterics.

'A taxi,' Raymond said. His shoulders were shaking. They were very happy.

'Do you write?' she asked Raymond.

'I try to, I'm on a great epic, you know, I hope. I've worked it out that if you want to write a great epic you just keep on writing and one day you've *got* an epic. But while I'm doing this I've got one or two little typing jobs which help to keep the wolf from the door.'

'He doesn't mean me,' Roger said. They both giggled again.

'What do *you* do, Mr. . . . ?' she asked Roger. 'I don't know your proper name.'

'Roger Hunter,' Raymond said. 'Antoine when he's working. He's a hairdresser.'

'Your hair would set a treat,' Roger said, looking at Julia. His was in excellent condition, she thought, beautifully cut with wispy bits low down on his neck, tendrils, and the same on his forehead. I should like to do his head too, except that his beauty lay in his eyes, and that wasn't possible with clay. 'I don't often have it done,' she told him, 'I'm afraid of looking different in the mirror. The last time I had it done was on my wedding day, and when I looked in the mirror it was a different girl. It's a queer sensation,' she shouldn't have said that, 'it's a peculiar sensation. You don't know how to behave when your face is different.'

'Most of my clients could do with being different,' Roger said, 'fat old cows.' They both laughed again.

'Would you like to see my workroom?' she asked.

'What do you work at?' They both said it together and then they put up their hands palm to palm and said, 'Pat-a-cake, pat-a-cake, baker's man.' They were very happy boys. She wondered what age they were. Eighteen or nineteen, she thought. Perhaps she could ask them later. 'I work with clay. I was just thinking what good models both of you would make, you're so beautiful. My workroom is in the attic so that I don't tramp the mess through the flat. Would you like to come and see it?'

'It's very kind of you, dear,' Raymond said, 'all right. Would you just nip into the kitchen, Roger, and turn down the gas under the lamb stew?' He said to Julia, 'We always do ourselves a proper meal. No scrappy bits. You can't keep your figure that way.'

They were very admiring. They looked carefully at

88

each head, and they read the poem. 'Is it a nursery rhyme?' Roger asked.

'In a kind of way.'

'That's where the money is,' Raymond said, looking bitter, 'if you could illustrate a children's book you'd be made. And even better if you could write it. I'm no good on children's stories. I've tried it several times but I can't ...' he now looked wistful, 'I don't know anything about children.'

'Very artistical,' Roger said. He had been considering for a long time, his head on one side. 'I like the gold paint. That gives it a touch of class.'

'Roger knows what he's talking about,' Raymond said, 'hairdressing is a minor art form, really, not to be sneezed at. He goes in for quite a lot of competitions, travels all over the country.'

'The girls are bitches,' Roger said, 'but I like it. I've to study faces just the way you've got to do, Mrs. Paton.'

'Who's that?' she said, looking over her shoulder.

'You, dear,' Raymond said.

'Oh, me! But I'm Julia!' They all giggled, and she thought that perhaps she had a sense of humour after all.

Roger said, 'You see, you've to model hair to the shape of a face, the style to suit the personality. You've to think it out.'

'You make people into other people?'

'No, I don't,' Roger said, 'I've just told you, you study the shape ...'

'It's gilding the lily, dear,' Raymond put in peacefully, 'but in your case there's no gilding required. If I may pass such a remark.'

'I don't mind. I'd like to be you to see what you think of me. You never know.'

'Why don't you ask your husband? He'd tell you, all right. Waiting for the chance, I shouldn't wonder.'

'It isn't important to me how I look. I'm concerned

with myself, trying to find out about me. Don't *you* ever puzzle?'

'Beauty is in the eye of the beholder,' Raymond said, which didn't seem to help, 'but in your case any eye which beholds you would say you were beautiful, isn't that so, Roger?'

'Yes,' he said, not looking, 'but girls are bitches.'

She liked them. They had coffee but no drinks, they didn't touch it, they said, and then they nosed round the flat like a couple of magpies, lifting and laying, admiring the Hi-fi, asked if they could go into the bedroom, looked at Lawrence's shirts and ties, opened his wardrobe.

'Ooh, this is a beauty.' Roger held Lawrence's fun shirt up in front of him. It was cotton voile with embroidered white flowers. 'A see-through.'

'He bought it for a laugh,' Julia said, 'he's got a pink tie to go with it.'

'Pink would be perfect,' Roger said. 'Well, when he gets tired of it, tell him to throw it in my direction.' They both laughed a lot at that.

The flat seemed very quiet when they went away. She washed up the coffee cups, but in spite of their frequent reference to their lamb stew, she didn't feel like cooking for herself. She turned on the television to make a noise. She usually liked it quiet, but this was a different type of quiet without Lawrence.

He would be in Amsterdam now. What time was it? Nine o'clock. Her small watch gleamed at her, a present from Lawrence ...

Roger and Raymond would be sitting down to their lamb stew together, and Lawrence and Kate . . . no pretence in the world could alter the fact that, being Lawrence, he would give Kate dinner.

When the television man had pointed out the map in his jovial manner and said good night, she turned the switch and watched the picture draw into a little round spot of light, and then, nothing. There was all tomorrow yet. Perhaps she would visit Mother and Father, perhaps...

She went into the bedroom and saw the white shirt where Roger had laid it down on a chair. She lifted it, putting her face against it for a moment, laid it down again and then went into the bathroom. Her face in the mirror looked tear-stained, but she hadn't been crying, surely? Perhaps when she had sat half-asleep in the chair? But she didn't remember, or what she had been thinking of. 'Beauty is in the eye of the beholder,' Raymond had said. But beauty was meaningless without Lawrence who delighted in it.

When she got into bed she curled herself into a ball with her hand under her cheek. Lawrence, I miss you . . . What are you doing? Are you sitting looking at Kate and thinking how pretty she is with that soft black hair and the wide mouth with the pink lipstick and the white teeth? To look at Kate's face when she was talking was interesting, it was mobile, expressions came and went. No good for sculpting. But it was a colourful face, the grey-green eyes, the pale brown skin, the dark hair, the pink lips.

And what would Kate see as *she* looked? Lawrence, Julia's Lawrence, with the kind eyes and the thin face and the black hair which had money spent on it unlike his wife's. Lawrence, Julia's Lawrence, no one else's . . . but it was after midnight. They wouldn't be sitting looking at each other. The dinner would be over . . .

In the morning she lay awake in bed feeling an unexplained sadness like a weight on her chest. Knowing that to get up would relieve it, she still lacked the energy. She lay motionless, her mind a heavy blank, refusing to form her fears into something cogent, and then, in a sudden burst of energy she threw back the clothes and got up. Immediately it was better. She put on her dressing-gown and went quickly up to the workroom where her salvation lay.

She hadn't consciously thought about it but she had to work on the head again. She had said to Lawrence it was finished but it wasn't. The line under the chin, she now confirmed as she looked at it, was too sharp. You only got that clearcut line in young people, boys, a child had a sloping line, a soft almost blurred line, there would not be this sharpness.

That was the difficulty here, that while working with clay she had still to convey a blurred outline, an unformed outline. Clay had its limitations. For instance, she couldn't ever do Roger because his only beauty lay in his eyes, and that beauty lay in their colour and the thick sweeping length of his eyelashes. You would have to have paint for that, load the brush, sweep it thickly too.

But she could improve the head. She turned it slowly on the turntable. She shouldn't have been in such a hurry to tell Lawrence that it was ready. It had to be perfect for Lawrence, 'Lawrence, I give this to you . . .'

She worked on without noticing the time. Somehow it went, somehow it was lunchtime and Lawrence had said he would be back in the early evening. She covered the head and went quickly downstairs.

What first? She was suddenly agitated. She would leave the kitchen meantime. There were dirty cups and the stove was dirty where the milk had boiled over leaving a thick wrinkled scum on the drip-plate. She had been too tired last night to wipe it. And there was the bedroom, the bed unmade, her clothes lying about, the drawers and wardrobes disturbed by Raymond and Roger in their magpie searching. 'Go ahead,' she had said, 'Lawrence wouldn't mind.'

No, the best thing to do was to run the bath and lay out clean clothes to wear, that chiffon dress which Lawrence liked so much. 'My nymphet,' he called her. She ran to the bathroom, turned on the tap, ran back. Strangely enough, she thought, I have never tried to tantalise Lawrence sexually, or dress to please him. It wasn't necessary. The deep comfort which she felt when he was with her was quickly fanned into love, a needy kind of love. Did she shock him at all? Should she then have been languorous, provocative, not responding immediately to the touch of his hands on her body, should she have been cool like the Lady of Shalott? But *she* hadn't been cool at all, and look what had happened to her, brought dead in a barge, dead of love. You could die of love. If Lawrence left her for someone else she would die of love.

Should she then be cool, calm, waiting, *La Belle Dame Sans Merci*? But it was no good thinking that now. She wanted Lawrence to have her quickly. 'Quickly, quickly,' she sometimes said, and he would stroke her brow, talking in that low lover's voice which sent long shafts of delight running through her body, 'Take it easy, darling.' But she couldn't, not with Lawrence. Julia's Lawrence. The telephone rang. She ran quickly, thinking he's in London, he's phoning to warn me, he'll be here soon.

'Lawrence!' she said with joy, and he answered.

'Hello, darling. What are you doing?'

'Just going to have a bath. Preparing for you. Then I'll start planning our dinner. I've got lots of things in the frig, and Lawrence, I had the two boys downstairs in last night. They were sweet. Roger is an expert hairdresser. Lawrence, why aren't you speaking?'

'Because you won't let me get a word in edgeways. Darling, I'm going to disappoint you. The director I had to see was off ill with a tummy upset and had to cancel his appointment. But he's promised he'll be in tomorrow morning. He's quite sure, just something he had eaten. Darling, I'll have to stay on another day. You won't mind?'

'Is Kate staying?'

'Well, I expect so. Couldn't you go to Wimbledon? It would pass the time for you. Darling, I'm sorry. It's unfortunate, I know, but having come so far I must see

93

this chap, get our business settled. You do see that, don't you?'

'I do see that,' she said.

'Have you kept yourself busy?'

'I've been working. I'm going to have a bath.' She remembered the running tap, 'I'll have to go, Lawrence.'

'There's no rush. Stay and talk to me.'

'I've left the bath tap on.'

'Oh, I see. All right, darling. Think of me?'

'Yes...'

'I'll think of you.'

'Yes, Lawrence ... goodbye.'

The water had overflowed, not very much but too much to wipe up easily. At least for the time being. She would have to do it, of course, but not immediately. She would creep into bed because she was really very cold, she would keep on her dressing-gown and after a time she would get up and face things. There was the kitchen too, and the dirty cooker, but she had a whole day and part of the next one to do it in ... plenty of time. She would curl up in a ball here, drawing her knees up to her chin.

The heat was like the sun ... Once, long ago, in the lane that ran down to Crawford's grandparents' house, she had found a nest. It had three blue eggs in it, but the mother bird had gone. She remembered vividly the intense speaking blueness of the eggs, their simplicity, the careless artifice of their arrangement amongst the twigs. She saw the little girl peering into the hedge, saw her curl up in the ditch quietly, waiting.

The mother bird arrived, harassed, a wisp of straw on her head, her feathers bedraggled with household cares. She perked her head round first, the eye a dark blue bead, and then hopped into the nest and sat on the eggs, moving her body to make herself comfortable. Her head perked round again.

The girl watched without being seen. Once her own

94

eye met the blue bead but she stayed quiet, quiet as quiet. She heard all the noises, absolutely all the noises, the small creak of branches, the grasshoppers rubbing their legs, and a far-off dog barking in the farm. She felt the sun on her head, but kindly, because it could not force itself fully through the thick interlace of the hedge.

'What are you lying there for?' Crawford said.

She rolled over and put her finger to her lips, but he didn't pay any attention. The sun was blotted out by him, her finger was still on her lips, holding back the scream...

'I'll sleep,' she said in the quiet room, 'if I sleep I can sleep one day away and then after that Lawrence will be nearly here.' But she must get up early because there was the cleaning and the wiping to be done and the cooking, but just for a little time she would let the sun warm her and forget about Amsterdam and Kate and Lawrence who said he loved her, Lawrence ... Crawford ... 'Crawford ...' she said aloud.

10

'What did you do after the appointment was cancelled?' Kate asked. They were in the bar of the American Hotel having cocktails.

'Looked for you, mostly,' he was always a charmer, 'you went running off like a scalded cat. Another drink?'

'All right, thank you. I'll have to watch that Dutch gin. I feel my head reeling.' And indeed she saw him through a rosy glow. Did you go to the Rijksmuseum?'

'Yes, wonderful. And, of course, the way they've done the Night Watch certainly enhances its impact. That long empty tunnel leading to it and the marvellous clarity of the lieutenant in yellow. The *shock*.'

'Yes, I went too.' She had only to shut her eyes to see the lieutenant in all his golden brilliancy. My life, she thought, has been a long empty tunnel leading to Lawrence. Dutch gin. 'After that I went to buy shoes. I've a passion for shoes.'

'I bought Julia a bracelet.'

'A diamond one? You've come to the right place.'

'Nothing so swish. Semi-precious stones in an antique setting. I think she'll like it.'

'Is it a peace offering for dining with me?'

'No, it isn't,' he looked embarrassed, 'I'm a big boy now and fairly civilised. I suppose I can ask you out to dinner without feeling it's wrong, or for that matter, having to go down on bended knees and confess to Julia.'

A waiter was at his elbow. 'Your table is ready, sir.'

'Good.' They got up. She shouldn't have said that. It was tactless, and bitchy. Dutch gin. She would have to watch it.

But she had started a train of thought. When they were seated and they had chosen their meal he said, 'Why didn't you dine with me last night?'

'I told you I had a headache. Flying sometimes does it. I told you I should have to go to bed with an aspirin and a good book.'

'When I've a headache I can't read.'

'This was a particular kind of headache, Dutch influence and misguided loyalty.'

'Who was the loyalty directed at, misguided or not?' He poured some wine.

'If that's as potent as their gin, go carefully, Lawrence. I'll be doing an "I'm a little Dutch girl" routine all round the room.' She put the backs of her hands together, smiled over them.

'A charming thought but you didn't answer my question.'

'It was directed at Julia, if you must know. I didn't like the thought of her sitting biting her nails at home

96

because we were dining together, and I wanted to say with conviction when I saw her that in fact we hadn't. There's nothing gives you the same conviction as truth.'

'Since you're such a female George Washington why did you accept tonight?'

'Well, you got me in a weak moment in the bar, and I thought, why rail against fate?' It's hard, she thought, damned hard. I should forget him and marry Richard. It would be so simple.

'You look particularly pretty tonight,' he said, 'you've fluffed out your hair.'

'That was another of the things I did today, had it fluffed out for me. I've a passion for foreign hairdressers, I feel I'm a challenge to them.'

'Had you been here before?'

'Amsterdam? Never.'

'Do you like it?'

She was pleased that the conversation had veered away from Julia. The gin and the wine had made her loquacious. 'It's like the Rembrandt, a city of strong light and shade, a city of chiaroscuro, and don't ask me how I delved that word up. It would be more in Julia's line,' and then aware that she had brought Julia into the conversation again she felt forced to ask, 'Is she with her parents?'

'No, she preferred to stay in the flat, and I didn't push her to go with them. After all, I shall be away from time to time, and she's best to get used to it right away. I hated to have to phone her today, though, and say I was held up.'

'Will she be lonely?'

'I don't think so. She spends a lot of time on her own. She's really a very solitary person.'

'Yes, she is, isn't she? She's not at all interested in women's chat, or clothes, I soon found. She's sweet. She asks you direct questions, unconventional ones . . .' She laughed, and I wish I were dead, she thought.

'What, for instance?'

'Well, it's silly mentioning it at all. She asked me if I enjoyed looking in a mirror! I thought she meant was I vain, and then I realised she wanted to know just that. She said it was something she absolutely didn't like, I remember her saying that, "absolutely didn't like". She's sweet,' she said again.

'She's right, of course. I've never seen her preening, and God knows she's beautiful enough to do a bit of preening.'

'Yes, she's beautiful. People turn in the street and look at her. Such a delicate kind of beauty . . .'

'Oh, she's healthy. She's got tremendous energy.'

Stop it, Kate, she thought as she spoke again, 'Did you know she was a solitary person before you got married?' It was a pity she had remembered what Richard had said about her . . . 'You develop antennae and when they're really quivering that means you're a good diagnostician. It's the best kind of intuition, seemingly spontaneous, but backed by reading and experience. Anyhow, mine are beginning to quiver . . .'

'In a way, yes,' Lawrence was saying, 'even on our honeymoon she sometimes disappeared,' his face was tender, 'she has solitary pursuits, almost like a child. She used to catch insects in the hotel pool. I found her a hollow stick with a lip. She has the tremendous concentration of a child, the self-absorption. Perhaps it's because she was an only child. There were two of us.'

'And four of us. I was knocked about by my three brothers.' There's something here, she thought, something *different* about this girl. I agree with Richard. I won't think further than that, I won't talk any more about her, we'll leave the subject of Julia now, let her be . . .

'You're a lucky man,' she said, 'having Julia.'

'Yes, I'm lucky.' The still tender look on his face was hurtful all right. Here, she thought, sitting across from

98

me in a strange hotel in a romantic city, is the one man I've ever wanted, and just when I had begun to think there was a chance, this girl, Julia, comes along and then he can't see anyone else but her.

'Are you having a sweet?' he asked.

'No, thank you.'

'Cheese?'

'No, again. I had it for breakfast.'

'A quaint local custom. I rather like it. How about a liqueur?'

She paused. 'I've drunk enough.'

'Oh, come on, Kate, you're a hard business girl, you can manage a liqueur?'

'If you say next that I'm as tough as old boots I'll . . . I'll . . .' She smiled at him.

'I wouldn't dream of saying that. I think you're very pretty. I've always thought so.' But not beautiful.

She looked at him. It was heartbreaking. She looked too long.

'What's wrong with you tonight, Kate?' He smiled and caught her hand.

'Wrong?' She was outraged at her stupidity. 'Wrong? Nothing. Don't hold my hand in public.'

'I believe you're shy! The hard business girl is shy!' He laughed at her.

'I've never been shy. Nothing makes me shy. Don't flatter yourself. If you persist in filling me up with drink so that I become owl-eyed I'm *still* not shy.'

'All right.' His smile was sweet. 'When we have our brandy and our coffee I'll take you out on the town. Perhaps you're in need of fresh air.'

'You must ask me first.'

'I shall, oh, I shall.' He smiled again, 'This is uncommonly nice, Kate, dear, dining tête-à-tête with you. I find you easy, always have done.'

'Like an old glove?'

'You're prickly tonight. Why?'

'Shall I tell you why?' For a moment she wondered what his face would look like if she said, 'Because I love you. There, I've said it, it's because I love you.' She bent her head to look intently at her plate. 'Delft?' She looked up at him, wide-eyed.

'Come on,' he said, he hadn't let go of her hand.

She shrugged. 'Well, it's because I'm feeling guilty which is surprising and ridiculous. I'm not saying this is the first time I've dined with a married man, but,' she moved, got her hand back, 'your Julia is remarkably persistent. Not in the usual way. I *feel* her here with us, which means, without being psychic, that she's thinking hard about us just now. Julia is the kind of girl you don't want to hurt, who is easily hurt . . .'

'You're wrong. Julia likes you. And she's not so vulnerable as you think. You haven't got on a pair of your new shoes, by the way?'

'No,' she said mystified.

'Good. Well, it's a fine night, we'll see what Amsterdam has to offer the stranded traveller. May I escort you?' He sketched a bow. What could she say?

Cities, she thought, walking in the thronged streets, become rave cities for me by passing a simple criterion. They must be good to walk about in at night. There was the tulip tree which she had seen in daylight, now like a burning bush in the heart of the city. There were the accommodating ladies sitting in their lit windows, if you have merchandise to sell you must display it. She was pleased to see that one was knitting. She thought that some of the sex-mad youth of England might look on that and ponder.

And now, with Lawrence hurrying her towards the sound of music, was an unexpected sight, a gigantic steam organ, a calliope, a fair in the middle of the city.

They were enchanted at their discovery, enchanted by the calliope's noise and splendour, its larger than life quality, the brilliance of its coloured electric light bulbs, its velocity. When they stood listening to its bangings and its crescendos, its piercing whistles and glissandos, Lawrence slipped his arm through hers, and she moved in pain.

'Come along,' he said like a boy, 'we're strangers here. Come on the roundabouts!'

'I can't,' she said, 'it would churn my gin and my wine and my brandy, and I should disgrace you for ever more.'

'Well, what about the water-buses? The poor man's gondola?'

'That I should like.'

She was feeling tipsily romantic, this was the Venice of the North. To sit beside him in the darkness, which had to be a velvet darkness, of course, would be a cheap thrill. She had no patience with herself. So what if he was the golden lieutenant, the flame-like figure who beckoned? It was all done by mirrors. And Julia didn't like mirrors.

She thought they were sitting too close together and she moved away. Lawrence looked down on her and put his arm round her again, smiling. Did he know he was her lieutenant, her crock of gold? He bent and gave her a swift friendly kiss on the cheek. 'Lovely, isn't it? I wish Julia could see it.' She breathed hard. She had to try not to be bitter.

The Venice of the North. And the houses lining the canals, Anne Frank's house, Rembrandt's house, the smallest house (a mere sliver wedged between two large ones), boat-houses, the size of the windows of the houses, 'Please to look,' the guide said, 'a former sign of affluence,' the landscape of Amsterdam at night was a cunning disposition of unequal houses, tall narrow houses (burgher-like and velvet-draped), reflected in the quiet waters of the canals. And a city of the unknown woman seen from the water-bus whose white cat stalked in the darkness amongst her geranium pots. She was desolated when they landed at the wharf and it was over.

Outside her door Lawrence kissed her and she let him, holding her body in check. Rembrandt-madness, Dutch gin-madness. He had kissed her because he thought it was expected of him, he had a man's outsize ego, he couldn't *not* kiss her lest she should be disappointed.

'I won't tell a soul,' she said, laughing lightly. But she shut the door firmly in his face.

'Julia!' he called, 'Julia, I'm back.' It had been a successful trip after all, he thought, putting his brief-case down in the narrow hall. He had cleared up the misunderstanding and Kate had been impressed. 'It isn't fair,' she had said in the plane coming back, 'women just don't have a chance.'

'Julia! Where are you, darling?' She had been quiet in the plane, dear Kate, as sound as a bell, Richard didn't know what he was missing . . . 'Julia!'

She couldn't be out. That would be too disappointing. There was a peculiar silence in the house as if someone was there and keeping quiet rather than an ordinary quietness. He became faintly agitated. His wife should be waiting for him.

He looked into the kitchen. There were dirty cups in the sink and the drip-plate of the cooker had been pulled halfway out. There was a mess of brown sticky sludge on it. Someone had begun to clean it and had been interrupted in the task.

He went into the sitting-room. Everything was all right here, and yet there was something, one or two of his records were half-out their sleeves and he was particular about his records, and there was a frowsty feeling as if it had missed the passage of human bodies to stir the air about, or that it should have a window open.

Poor darling, he thought, she must have got fed up on her own and gone to Wimbledon. It wasn't like her to leave things in a mess. Her passion for scouring was a private joke between them, 'my Mrs. Mop,' he called her.

He opened the bedroom door into a half gloom. The curtains were still drawn, and there were clothes strewn on the chairs. Julia was in bed. He could see the curve of her back and the glint of her fair hair spread out like a fan on the pillow. A great fear took hold of him. There was nothing intrinsically wrong about an untidy house, or for that matter a girl who was in bed at five o'clock in the afternoon. She could have been ill, 'her pain', she called it when she was wan-cheeked and hollow-eyed. 'My poor little Julia, my poor little woman.'

But this was a different kind of fear. His heart ached with it. 'Julia,' he said softly, touching her shoulder, 'it's Lawrence. Julia, darling, are you all right?'

She moved. She turned over to face him and put out her hand. He took it in his. 'What are you doing there, you lazy girl?' he asked. He winced at the hollow heartiness of his voice.

'What time is it, Lawrence?' Her voice was faint.

'Five o'clock.'

'What day is it?'

'Oh, Julia, you know perfectly well. It's Tuesday.' Again the fear took hold of him and he tried to speak lightly. 'I've been round the house. It's in a hell of a mess, not at all like you. Has something happened? Have you been ill?'

She shook her head. Great tears stood in her eyes, but she made no sound. He gathered her into his arms, speaking softly. 'You haven't been ill?'

He felt her head shake. Again the fear gripped at his guts. 'Well, I'll tell you what I'll do. I'll go and make some tea and clean up the place a bit. And afterwards while you're dressing I'll make some food for us. Will that do?'

'Lawrence,' she said, she sounded heartbroken, 'the bath ran over.'

'Yes, you told me,' he said, 'on the phone. But that was a whole day ago.' He stared at her. 'You turned the tap off?'

'Yes, I turned it off,' she began to sob, 'but not soon enough. And I didn't wipe up the mess.'

'Was it bad?'

'I think it was bad.'

'I'll go and see.' He went into the bathroom and saw that the floor was damp but not very wet. Most of the water must have seeped away. He bit his lip but went quickly back to her. 'It could be worse,' he said. 'Put on your slippers and have a bath while I make the tea.'

He pulled the bedclothes back and he saw she was wearing her dressing-gown. It was hopelessly creased and there was a stale smell from her. 'Darling,' he said, frightened again, 'you've been ill. I'll ring Richard and see if he'll come up to have a look at you.'

'There's no need for Richard.' Her face was sullen.

'But what's a doctor for? No girl stays in bed unless there's something wrong.' He still couldn't believe that she had been so disturbed at him staying on another night that she had lain in bed until now. He was fresh from Kate, and he thought, Kate wouldn't do that in a thousand years.

He ran the bath and helped her into it. He thought that she was pitifully thin, thinner than when he had left two days ago. He noticed that her hands were cold and blue at the finger-tips. 'My poor darling,' he said, filled with concern, feeling somehow to blame, 'in you get. You'll soon be nice and warm.'

The bell rang. He went quickly to the door and opened it. Perhaps it would be Richard dropping in, which would indeed be fortuitous. But it was the boy from downstairs who stood there, the little queer. He looked white and frightened.

'Mr. Paton? Oh, I'm awfully glad you're back. We've been terribly worried. We noticed the water coming through our ceiling and we've rang and rang. We thought Mrs. . . . Julia, must have gone away.'

'No, she's been ill,' he said. 'Is the damage bad?'

'Yes, it's bad. Roger did the ceiling only last week for me, such a pretty colour, duck-egg blue. It's been dripping through though it's stopped now, but the plaster's flaking off in some parts.'

'I'm very sorry. It's entirely our fault. Look, Mr. . . .'

'Raymond.'

'Mr. Raymond . '

'No, it's Mr. Mills.'

'Look, I'm rather pressed just now. I don't want to leave my wife alone. Would you get in the decorators or whoever you need and I'll pay for the damage done?'

'I hate to bother you, but Roger and I were just saying we couldn't be blamed. Could we? You see, a bill for that would floor us, really floor us, just when we're getting on our feet. I write, you know. I've worked it out that if I just keep on . . .'

'Mr. Mills, excuse me, but I must shut the door on you. Most rude. All bills to me.'

'It's awfully kind of you. Is Julia, your wife, all right? We had such a good time with her on Sunday.' His white face was anxious.

'Yes, I think she'll be all right. My deepest apologies. Good night.' He shut the door firmly on Raymond's frightened smile.

He tore back to the bathroom. Julia was lying back in the bath, her eyes closed, but there was a hint of colour in her cheeks. She hadn't soaped herself.

'Lazy girl,' he said, he got her face cloth and began to wash her, thinking again how thin she was. 'Raise your arm. Now the other one. That's the ticket. Now this leg . . .' When he had finished he helped her out and wrapped her in a large towel.

'Give yourself a brisk rub,' he said, 'and I'll go and get your bed ready for you.'

'But you said I had to get up.' She smiled at him, and it was the old Julia whom he loved, 'I don't want to go back to bed, I'm fine now. I don't know what went wrong. The time was hazy, it slipped past. Once or twice I thought I heard a rattle at the door but I thought it would be the wind in the trees.'

'What trees?'

She smiled brilliantly. 'Stupid me. Of course there are no trees. But there are round Corfe Cottage.'

'It would be the boy downstairs. Some of the water has seeped through to his ceiling, but he was very understanding. He was more worried about you.'

'Was it Raymond or Roger?'

'Raymond.'

'He and his friend were so nice. We had such a good time . . . before you telephoned . . .'

'Rub yourself dry.' He hurried to the bedroom and flung back the bedclothes to enable him to straighten the under-sheet. There was a book lying half underneath the pillow, and he took it out. It was one of her exercise books, she used a lot of them for drawing in. She would obsessionally draw the same thing over and over again, the leg of a chair, the corner of the room, until she was pleased with it. He supposed it was a form of doodling.

It fell open as he lifted it and he saw the words rather than consciously read them.

'Far away in a plane Lawrence and Kate like the sea-gull like the bird in the hedge Crawford wants to see the eggs and Lawrence says hello on the telephone and I like his dark hair and his eyes because they belong to me only I wish he would stay and stay but there is Roger and Raymond and they giggle and are pretty like Kate who is not a friend they liked the shirt but I don't think it would suit Crawford . . .'

He was stunned. Crawford, he thought, a name beginning with 'C'. What is this obsession she has with this damned Crawford? Fear took hold of him, worse than

106

ever, and he felt his face twist. He looked up and she was standing in the doorway. She had a towel wrapped round under her arms and across her breast and she looked very beautiful.

'What are you doing, Lawrence?'

'Making the bed. Pop in.'

'That's my book.'

'Is it? It fell out from under the pillow. Come on, hop in.'

'It's my drawing-book.'

'Well, take your old drawing-book.' He thrust it under the pillow and turned towards her.

She smelled fresh and sweet. He let the towel drop and pressed her body to his. He pushed her hair back from her brow and saw the wide candid eyes, 'You must have picked up a bug. Poor you.' That was the explanation, she was fevered. People talked nonsense when they were fevered. But her eyes were clear and cool. Ah, just a minute . . . Was she pregnant? *That* was it. Relief flooded through him. Pregnancy made girls act strangely at times.

He lifted the fresh nightdress he had laid out and put it over her head. He tucked her in bed securely, taking a pride in turning back the top sheet over the blankets, pulling it taut to remove the creases. 'I'm going to look after you *real* good.' He clowned.

'Lawrence, you're funny.' She laughed up at him.

'I'll get your tea now, wife.' He kissed her. Mother-to-be. He didn't say that.

He went out of the room and shut the bedroom door. He went quietly into the sitting-room and eased the telephone receiver off its cradle. Richard would be in his surgery. He flicked at the pad, found the number, and dialled as softly as he could.

A woman's voice answered. 'Doctors Cantilever, Jones and Lewis.' Jones would be the one who had been so keen to have Richard, a fellow Welshman.

'May I speak to Dr. Lewis?'

'Is it a patient calling?'

'Yes, it's rather urgent. I think he'll speak to me. Paton's my name.'

'I'll put you through.' She sounded grudging.

He heard Richard's voice. 'Richard, it's Lawrence here. Sorry to bother you. I've just got back from Amsterdam, and, well, to tell you the truth, I found Julia in bed, not herself at all.' That was true enough, God knew.

'What do you think is wrong?'

'You're the doctor.' Again the fear shook him. 'The place was untidy, uncared for. She had let the bath run over.'

There was a pause. He thought over what he had said and was appalled at the innocuousness of it. He was just going to apologise when Richard said, 'I shouldn't worry about it too much, Lawrence.'

'It sounds stupid now. I was alarmed . . . Do you think she could be pregnant?'

'Do you?'

'Well, frankly, no. She hasn't been using the Pill, but I've been careful. I felt we ought to wait a little, let her settle down. The Wimbledon doctor wasn't too keen to prescribe the Pill for her. I didn't ask why.'

'Maybe you've been careless, dear boy. Look, I'll slip round after the surgery and see her. Okay?'

'Thanks.'

'Had a good trip?'

'Yes, very good.'

'Did Kate behave herself?'

'She always does. Worse luck.'

'See you.' Richard hung up.

When Lawrence opened the door to Richard, he looked cheerful. They shook hands. 'Good of you to come, Richard,' and then, lowering his voice, 'she seems all right now. Would you mind just pretending it's a social call?'

'Okay. I'm glad she's better.' He followed Lawrence into the sitting-room.

Julia was sitting on a low stool in front of the television set. Her head bent on her slender neck was flower-like. He was struck again by her beauty, and yet, he thought, it's a beauty without . . . without what? Sex-appeal? She looked up, saw Richard and got to her feet, smiling brilliantly. 'Oh, Richard, how nice of you to drop in! Isn't it nice, Lawrence?'

'Great. Sit down, Richard. What will you have to drink?'

'A whisky and soda if you don't mind. I was on my way home. Thought I'd look in to see you both. How are you, Julia?'

'Oh, fine!' Her eyes strayed towards the television set. Lawrence went over and turned it off.

'No complaints?'

'No, I am absolutely all right. Lawrence was a bit annoyed when he came back and found the place in a mess, but I was just a little off-colour while he was away. I didn't get round to it.'

'What was wrong?'

'Oh, nothing very much.'

'Would you like to tell me about it?'

She shook her head. 'You're as bad as Lawrence. There's no need.' Richard took the drink from Lawrence, said, 'Thanks,' and their eyes met for an instant. Lawrence nodded. Richard knew he was going to make a hash of it. 'Sometimes, I'm not suggesting this for a moment, but sometimes women feel a bit off in the first stages of, er, pregnancy . . . you're not going to gladden the old man's heart?'

'Would it, Lawrence?' Her eyes sought his.

'I'm easy.'

'No,' she shook her head, 'I absolutely know I'm not pregnant, Richard.'

'Well, you should know. But if you feel seedy . . . or anything . . . come round to the surgery any day and I'll give you a check-up. I might even put you on to a good tonic. You're too thin.'

'Am I too thin, Lawrence?'

'Well, she's thin in the right places,' he smiled at Richard, 'if you know what I mean.'

Julia laughed. 'Please don't talk about me any more. It's terribly embarrassing, and I'm quite all right, really I am. I think I had got over-tired and it seemed a good time to rest while Lawrence was in Amsterdam.'

Well, you couldn't say fairer than that, Richard thought. He said, 'I phoned Kate today. I gather that the trip was a success from the business point of view.'

'Yes, it was. We had to stay over another day but we both had plenty to do. I told Kate she would never get through the Customs with the amount of shoes she bought.'

'She did.' Richard laughed. 'I've got a date with her tonight to go and see them.'

'I'd love to see Kate,' Julia said, 'and we've heaps of food. I didn't eat any while Lawrence was away. If you could bear to share her, phone her up and we'll have plates on our laps. It would be fun.'

'It's too much bother for you when you've been feeling unwell.'

'Aren't doctors the limit? Go on, phone her, Lawrence?' She appealed to him, 'Isn't it a good idea?'

'Perhaps they want to be alone.'

'You must say so, Richard.'

'*I* might but *she* doesn't. All right, Julia, thanks. I'll give her a ring if I may. We won't stay too long and tire you.'

'But I'm untirable, I'm untirable absolutely. Now sit down there and ring Kate and I'll go into the kitchen. It will be cold, Richard, the sweet too. Honestly, you're doing us a great favour helping us to eat up the food. Have we got wine, Lawrence?'

'Yes, heaps. I'll see to that. On you go, darling.' Even Richard could see the love in his eyes, but his feet were firmer on the ground, 'Perhaps you should wait till you see if Kate is coming?'

'All right.' She stood at the door. It's the *fine* quality of her beauty, Richard thought, smiling at her and lifting the receiver. He dialled Kate's number, I shouldn't want a wife like that, I should be afraid she would break . . . 'Hello, Kate, this is your ever-faithful and unrebuffed admirer speaking.'

'Which one?' Her voice had depth, you knew there was a fair amount of *woman* behind it.

He laughed, 'I didn't know I had any competition. Look, I'm in the Patons. Julia has offered us food. Would you like to come round?'

He listened. He looked at Lawrence while he listened. Kate was saying, 'I don't think it's a good idea, Richard. I had a feeling all the time I was away that Julia was worried about it. I'm sure it would be tactless to turn up.'

'The reverse.' He smiled at Julia and Lawrence again. I should have liked to say, he thought, that she was quite right, that Julia *had* been upset, that she was now over-compensating like mad . . . He smiled again at the two of them.

'Richard,' Kate was saying, 'can't you speak freely?'

'No.'

'Do you think I should come?'

'Yes.'

'All right. But don't blame me if she goes after me with

a hatchet. Does she appear quite friendly?'

'Yes, but,' he said.

'There has been a little trouble?'

'Mmmh.'

'All right. Say thanks and that I'll be there in half an hour.'

'Would you like me to pick you up?'

'No. I'll walk. And, Richard, we shan't stay long.'

'Okay. Suits me. 'Bye.'

'That's fine,' he said, smiling at Julia, 'she says she'll be delighted.'

'Oh, good!' She was radiant. 'Well, I'll leave you two to have a natter while I'm busy. Tell him not to worry, Richard.' Her eyes were clear, candid. Were they also appealing?

'I'll tell him.'

When she was in the kitchen Richard said, 'She seems perfectly all right.'

'Yes, she does. You think I was imagining half of it?'

'You could be. You're in love with the girl, aren't you?'

'Need you ask?'

'No, but you're in the precarious state of loving. The first few months are difficult, they tell me. This question of adjustment...'

'Yes, I see that.' Their eyes met and Richard thought, it's no good fobbing him off. You'd better give him something to grasp.

'Look, Lawrence,' he got up and closed the door, 'I think you must face the fact that Julia is, well, shall we say, highly-strung, for want of a better word, but I don't want to bemuse you with jargon.' He waved a hand, 'Perhaps a little more emotional than most, perhaps a little unconventional by ordinary standards because they don't recognise the norm, perhaps not, anyhow it's the *vulnerability* which is important. You know how we talk of some people having a lower threshold of pain than others. It's all a question of growing a thick enough skin

against the "slings and arrows of outrageous fortune."
One has to do it for survival in this world. Some people
never do. The gifted ones very often, and Julia is
gifted. They've to pay a toll.'

Lawrence nodded.

'Marriage. Well, I'm not an expert but it can be traumatic. The common clay generally take to it like a duck to
water, but others, like Julia, might find it a bit of a
strain. They might lose their mental equilibrium for a
little.'

'Would you think my going away perhaps tipped this
balance?'

'It might have done. She would miss you. Is she very
dependent on you?'

'I think so.'

'Could she be jealous of Kate?' He decided to come
right out with it.

'I had thought of that.'

'Did you reassure her that there was nothing to it?'

'No, it didn't come up.'

'*Is* there anything, Lawrence? I ask you as a man, not
a doctor.'

'Good grief, no! I like Kate, I think I even love her in
the best possible way, but Julia, with Julia, it's different...'

And I hope you're speaking the truth, Richard
thought. Because by God, I think she's attracted to *you.*
He spoke, 'Well, that's all right. Just remember the vulnerability and treat her like fine china for a time. Even
her appearance is a giveaway, the thinness, the slender
limbs, the delicate skin, the delicate beauty. She's
asthenic.' A thought struck him. 'Do you know anything
of Julia's background?'

'Well, it's pretty good, rather opulent, as a matter of
fact.'

'The parents are stable?'

'Oh, God, yes, Grant is very fine, kind, the best of

men. Lydia is rather more concerned with appearances, but she's got all the obvious virtues. I shouldn't say there was a tremendous rapport between Julia and her all the same.'

'There wouldn't be.' Not with anyone, he thought, except with Lawrence, her protector as well as her lover. 'Do you know anything of her antecedents?'

'Very little. Grant, I believe, had one sister who died at forty. Unmarried, I think. I remember Julia mentioning it. Is that important?'

Richard shrugged. 'It might be important to know why she didn't marry and why she died, but,' he had seen Lawrence's face, 'there's absolutely no need for a case history.' Nor to push this too far.

'Well, old man,' he said, 'there it is. I shouldn't worry. Gifted, nervous children make gifted nervous people when they grow up. They're ten-a-penny, and we couldn't do without them.'

'What about a family, Richard? You don't think she's pregnant?'

'Not for a second. But as regards the family, if I were you I wouldn't push that idea at the moment, let her have a year or two to settle down. After that . . .' The door bell went and he thought, bless you, Kate, you would arrive at the right moment. He heard Julia's clear voice, 'That will be Kate, Lawrence. Will you go? My hands are wet.'

Lawrence got up and Richard heard him at the door. 'Sweet Kate! Can't you stay out of my hair?' He suffered a sickening twist of jealousy.

He heard her laughter. 'Honestly, such arrogance!' How normal she sounded, how normal she *was*.

She came breezing into the room and said, 'Hi, Schweitzer.'

'Hi, globe-trotter.'

'Don't you two kiss when you meet?' Lawrence asked, behind her. 'Here, Kate, let me have your coat.'

'No, I daren't,' she said, as he helped her off with it, 'he'd be off like a laser beam to get a Special Licence.'

'You could do a lot worse.'

'That's what I keep telling her,' Richard said.

Julia came into the room. 'Kate, I'm glad you could come!' They didn't kiss either, 'Isn't this a good idea? We'll all sit round with plates on our knees and you can tell Richard and I all about Amsterdam.'

'What we saw of it. We weren't there on holiday, you know. It's very decent of you to feed us, Julia. It's my turn. I really will get round to it soon.'

'But I've got much more time than you. Would you like to come into the kitchen and help me with the plates? Lawrence, pour out the wine, please.' Now, there's a funny thing, Richard thought, she never uses an endearment. Is it significant? Because it makes her different? He dismissed it.

Lawrence got a bottle from a cupboard and took four glasses from the shelf above. 'I'll never be able to understand women,' he said.

'I go along with that.'

'Julia's very fond of Kate. You can see it. And you thought that perhaps...'

The girls came back, bearing a plate in each hand. There was a little flurry as they settled down. Julia's eyes were intensely blue, Richard noticed, there was the same radiance as he had noticed at her wedding, an inner excitement, such beauty, such *unearthly* beauty ... he didn't know why he felt uncomfortable.

The food looked delicious. There had been, to his eyes, a tremendous amount of care spent on the salad which went with the cold chicken. The tomatoes were cut into water-lily shapes and stuffed, the radishes were like rose-buds, there were hard-boiled eggs with their insides whipped into whorls topped with anchovies. If this girl had been in bed and in a mess when Lawrence got home she must have moved like greased lightning when she got up. But then she was a trained cook. He gave it up. 'This is lovely,' he said. He raised his glass to her.

'She's a Cordon Bleu, you know.' Lawrence stuck out his chest.

'Is there no end to your cleverness, Julia?' Kate said, smiling at her. 'Honestly, you make me feel like a bucolic peasant. You'll probably get shredded turnip when you come to see me.'

'In that case I don't think I'll marry you,' Richard said, chancing his arm.

'Try asking me.' Looking at them he thought the contrast between the two girls was striking. Kate's hair was brushed and whirled off her face, Julia's hung like a curtain. Sitting close beside her he thought the delicacy of her skin was remarkable. Kate's, opposite, was creamy but healthy, with some warmth. Then there was a toughness about her, perhaps the quick movements of her head, her healthy interest in what everyone said, her quick, accurate comments. You would have to go far, he thought, to see two prettier girls, but give me Kate every time for her lasting properties. Give me Kate . . . He saw her look at Lawrence and there was the sickening lurch of jealousy again. If she would only look at *him* like that he would be the happiest of men.

'Have you told Kate about my escapade, Lawrence?' Julia asked.

'What escapade, darling?'

'Letting the bath run over. Wasn't it terrible, Kate? When Lawrence phoned me saying that he would have to stay over another night I forgot about the water being turned on. It went through the floor which is, of course, the ceiling of Raymond and Roger who live downstairs.' She laughed, throwing her head back.

'I can't feel it was so hilarious for Raymond and Roger, whoever they are,' Kate said.

'No, it wasn't.' Julia immediately sobered, 'But it's so funny in some ways! Perhaps they had to sit round the table with their umbrellas up. If you knew them you'd see the funniness too, they're so sweet, and so loving, they'd be such a funny little pair with their umbrellas up . . .'

'I'm making good the damage,' Lawrence spoke shortly, 'we all make mistakes.' Yes, Richard thought, but we don't all see the funny side of them. Was it bizarre, or was it just a sense of humour? If you're uncomfortable there's something *there*, but leave it, leave it . . .

Julia smiled at Kate, 'Did you absolutely love Amsterdam, Kate?'

'Yes, I did. I'd love to go back again. It's quite beautiful. And cosmopolitan. I shouldn't mind seeing it in tulip time if it wouldn't be too banal.'

'What did you see?'

'The canals, of course. The Rijksmuseum, especially the Night Watch. I bought some photographs of it. I'll let you have one. You'd be interested.' She spoke to Richard, 'Hold my plate, ducky, please.' She opened her bag, brought out some postcards, handed one to Julia, 'It's in a dramatic setting, and this figure here,' she pointed, 'the lieutenant. He's dressed in a glorious singing yellow, quite unforgettable. You'd appreciate it, Julia.'

'Did you see it, Lawrence?' Julia asked. 'Thank you, Kate. May I keep this?'

'Yes, not with Kate. Good God,' he said, 'I brought you a present! I've been so worried . . . I mean, I've been so busy . . .' He went into the bedroom and came back with a little box in his hand. 'This is one-upmanship, if ever,' he said, grinning at Richard. 'Now you'll have to go and buy something for Kate.'

'Like an engagement ring? Anyhow,' he said, smiling at Kate, 'it should have been the other way round.'

'Poor ickle soul. As a matter of fact, *I* did bring you something to shut you up. Cuff-links.'

'Thanks!' He smiled with love on her, and she smiled back openly, fondly.

Lawrence put the bracelet over Julia's hand. It was a little big, and Richard thought it was too heavy for such a frail wrist. 'It's beautiful,' she said, 'I absolutely think it's beautiful and I adore you.' She put her cheek against his hand for an instant and Richard saw the unashamed, tender look in his eyes. Well, good luck, he thought, good luck to you, Lawrence. You've got a broad enough back.

It was a happy evening. Lawrence, relieved of his anxiety, was an excellent host, and Richard and Kate stayed later than he had intended because they were all talking so much. That is, Kate, Lawrence and Richard. The three of them had agile minds and catholic tastes. But when Richard saw that gradually Julia was being left out of the conversation, when he saw her eyes huge in the pale face, he thought, the child's had enough, and was surprised to find himself thinking, 'the child.' In any case, he had his own fish to fry, to put it bluntly, with Kate.

He said to her going down the stairs, 'If you care to come to my flat I'll do you a quick rape.'

She laughed, 'I'm not that desperate.'

'But, will you come back?' He tried to stop the pleading in his voice.

'Dear Richard,' she touched his arm, 'all right, I'll come back. I'm too wide-awake to sleep. I kept thinking that Julia might heave a saucepan at my head any minute.'

'No danger of that. She likes you.'

'Fat lot you know about women. She was probably seething underneath.'

'I don't think Julia's like other women. I think she likes you. I honestly think she's got an *attachment* to you. You'd be doing her a good turn if you remained friends with her.'

'Well, I'd like to, of course,' she looked doubtful, 'Richard, a long time ago you said something about your antennae. Were they quivering tonight?'

He had regretted that remark. A doctor, even with the girl he loved, should watch out about discussing patients, especially ones you weren't sure about. It had been all right in Leo Susskind's case. He had told him about Julia, expounding it as a hypothetical case, and Leo had given him a lot of useful information. But in the end you had to wait and see. 'No,' he said now, shortly. Kate was the wrong person to tell because she was emotionally involved with Lawrence. Not to put too great a point on it, she loved him. His antennae had quivered there all right.

'Kate,' he said, 'I'm tired of Lawrence and Julia. Haven't we all got problems?'

'That's true enough.'

They had reached his car. He opened the door. 'Hop in. We'll be back in my place in two ticks.'

'I don't think . . .'

'I want you to.' He felt his face grim as he took his place beside her, 'You can surely throw me a bone occasionally.'

She laughed and kissed his cheek. 'Poor Fido.'

In the flat he put his arms round her and kissed her and she let him. But it wasn't there. He released her. 'I'll get us some drinks,' he said, 'have a seat.'

'Gin for me, then,' she said, 'a double.'

He raised his eyebrows, went to the cupboard, poured out the gin. He had to drive her home. He was parsimonious with his own.

'Look, Kate,' he said, placing a table, putting the drinks on it, sitting beside her on the divan, 'I'm doing well in this job. Couldn't we get married? I'd have no territorial claims on you. You could go on working as long as you liked.'

'No,' she said, 'it isn't possible.'

He didn't reply. There was nothing to say. A heavy heart. He had often read the phrase. His heart was heavy. He knew what it meant. After a time he said, 'It's hopeless, isn't it?' He had his glass in his hand.

She took his drink, placed it on the table beside her own, pushed him back amongst the cushions, half-lying on top of him.

'Who's raping whom now?' he asked, surprised.

'Make love to me, Richard.'

'To help you to forget?'

'Just do it, Richard. Don't talk.'

He did, but he was ashamed. A deep burning shame was there all the time. No one likes to make love to a girl who has tears streaming down her face. For someone else.

12

And then, springing on the heels of autumn, it seemed, it was Christmas. The hiatus had been filled by Julia with shopping expeditions, from early November the flat was in a flurry of coloured paper and ribbon. She spent hours on wrapping the presents she had bought, tying intricate ribbon bows. One by one as they were finished she would show them to Lawrence and he would be struck by her artistry. There was a rightness about everything she did, the colour contrasts were right, the disposition of the ribbon bows, she had an unerring eye for colour and detail.

'People just tear them open and spoil all your good work,' he said to her, but she didn't agree. 'It's a work of love, I put love into it, they feel it at the first sight of the parcel, they'll open it tenderly, with love.'

Lawrence doubted this and was thankful she hadn't too many to do. There was her father and mother, two school friends to whom she wrote but never saw, their children, the Wards, who were her mother's friends,

Judy Thomson, their married daughter and her two children, Raymond and Roger downstairs, Richard and Kate, even Maggie, his secretary. His own was carefully hidden. At least he felt that it was a welcome change from her incessant preoccupation with her clay heads upstairs.

They were going to Corfe Cottage for Christmas with Lydia and Grant. Julia had told him they always did this, and he was looking forward to it. They had only been once since they were married, and it had been such a weekend of rain that all he remembered was a feeling of dampness in the bedsheets and Julia looking blue and cold. Her circulation was poor.

But she was well just now. The colour and glitter of impending Christmas appealed to her. They walked down Regent Street one night to see the lights, with Julia hanging on his arm like a child. They window-shopped for her present, a fur coat. Once when Richard rang him to enquire about her health he was able to say that he had never seen her look better, that she was even looking well-fed.

'Good news,' Richard had said. He told Lawrence that he was on duty at Christmas because the other partners had children and it was only fair that they should have the chance to spend it with them. Kate was going to Cheltenham.

Kate came into his room one day to talk about the Frankfurt Book Fair, but Maggie was there and they had stuck to business. Maggie had got up to go but Kate had stayed her with her hand. 'Don't budge, Maggie, this is for your shell-like ears too,' and had launched into an account of someone from Norway who had bought two books for publication.

At the door she said, 'I don't suppose you'll be going to Cheltenham at Christmas?'

'No, I'm afraid not. There's nothing there for me now, Kate. We're going down to Dorset with Julia's parents.'

'Lovely,' she said, 'jingle bells.'

He thought she looked paler than usual, and when their eyes met over Maggie's head that hers looked sad. When he was dictating the thought of them came back to him. Anything which happened to Kate affected him, he found himself thinking with surprise. He cared about her happiness, she deserved to be happy. But when he told himself that it would be a good thing if she and Richard got married, he found himself resenting the thought.

The day came when they were due to go down to Dorset. He had to go into the office for an hour in the morning, and he packed the car the night before. Julia would call for him and at the same time distribute the presents.

Maggie was taciturn, only just polite. She had very few social graces, and she seemed ill-at-ease in Julia's presence. But then she had always been an awkward girl. Only he had seen her possibilities when she was in the typing department and had her promoted. He knew she had an intense loyalty to him, but then he remembered intercepting her admiring gaze when Kate had been in the room. And yet Julia had never looked lovelier, in her new fur coat which he had persuaded her to wear, and an absurd kind of Cossack cap perched on her head.

'I've got something for Kate too,' she said. 'Shall I go and give it to her?'

'Yes, she'd like that.' He smiled at Maggie to include her in their happiness. She said ungraciously, when Julia was out of the room, 'Mrs Paton shouldn't have gone to all the trouble,' she nodded towards the parcel, 'it's too much.'

'She likes doing it. Besides, you don't know what's inside.' He decided that she was getting sour in her old age, or perhaps she would rather have had the fiver he generally gave her. Well, she would get that too.

He went along to Kate's office and found her laughing with Julia.

'This absurd wife of yours, Lawrence,' she looked up, 'she's gone to the trouble of buying me some intimate garments, she says coyly. But I've not to open it until Christmas.' She looked at Julia. 'How did you know my size?'

'I just looked.' Julia was sitting on the edge of her desk, swinging her legs. Her fur coat looked opulent, even overpowering in the small room. 'I know exactly your size.'

'She uses her artistic eye,' Lawrence said, 'don't forget she's used to measuring and assessing, aren't you, my love?'

'Yes, I do it all the time. I could draw a picture of Kate.'

'Gosh, that's quite disturbing,' Kate said, 'we've all got our figure secrets, and here are you going about with X-ray eyes.' She put her hand on her chest. 'You've probably spotted that I'm like a washer-woman!'

'Nonsense, Kate,' he said, 'you're just right. Isn't she, Julia?'

'Right for Kate.'

He thought he might have been indiscreet. 'I think we ought to be pushing on,' he said, 'the sky's darkening over. Perhaps we'll have snow in Dorset.'

'All right.' Julia got off the desk. 'Well, happy Christmas, Kate.' They didn't kiss or shake hands.

'Happy Christmas. My present's in the post, so mundane and banal that I hate to think of it, but given with my love.'

'Happy Christmas, Kate.' Lawrence kissed her because he was the kind of man who kissed women he liked. Her cheek was cold. Kate, he thought, you're upset, but when their eyes met he was relieved to see that she was smiling. 'Happy Christmas, you. I'll give your love to Cheltenham.'

'Yes, do that.'

He didn't speak when they were walking towards the lift. 'What's wrong?' Julia asked.

'Nothing.' He didn't know what was wrong with him, a sudden unexplained sadness, nothing at all.

Corfe Cottage was warm and comfortable with Lydia at the helm. The central heating was singing, and there was a pleasant smell of roasting and baking for the two days preceding Christmas. Grant helped. He was handy in the kitchen. 'I'm the sauce chef,' he told Lawrence, 'what's your forte?'

'I consider myself the unhandiest man in Christendom, I'm afraid I'll have to be dogsbody. I'll start by shovelling the snow from the front door. At least its traditional.'

Because it had snowed after all. Not a great fall, but whereas in London it would have been swept or melted away in a few hours, here it lay, as he said, 'deep and crisp and even' in the fields, round the house, and in the lane leading to the church.

The Wards, the friends of Lydia and Grant, were in residence in the house at the foot of the lane. There was a toddler of three called Sue, their grand-daughter, whom Lawrence privately adored. And a baby who was being brought up on spartan lines because often there was a pram in the snowy garden.

'I can't understand girls who can't hold their husbands,' Lydia said to Lawrence, when he was sitting on the edge of the kitchen table sampling Julia's batch of mince pies.

'Perhaps he wasn't worth holding,' he said, 'they say you don't know anyone properly until you live with them.'

'That's for sure.' There was a chuckle from Grant who was stirring at the stove in a butcher's apron.

'Lawrence is even nicer than I thought,' Julia said. He blew her a kiss.

'Still, an effort can be made,' Lydia said, and then, quickly, 'you and Julia at any rate are happy.'

'God, yes, we're happy all right.'

'I'm going upstairs to change,' Julia said, 'don't talk about me while I'm gone.'

'As if we would.' When she was out of the room he said to Lydia, 'She's looking very well just now. Sometimes she's . . . frail. Was she, er, difficult as a child?'

'In what way?' He thought her eyes looked guarded.

'Well, sometimes I get the impression that she's not fit to cope with the hurly-burly of everyday life, that she's easily . . . cast down, and then, although I buy her all kinds of goodies she never puts on weight. She burns it up.'

'People vary, Lawrence.' Grant's voice was understanding, 'Julia will never be, well, a good armful, but then I think you would look for slightly more than that.'

This conversation, he thought, has suddenly assumed the same proportions as that of a man who has bought the wrong goods and brings them back to the shop to see if they can be exchanged. He noticed that Grant went on stirring, and he wondered if he was reading too much into everything. Julia was his love, wasn't she, and didn't he adore her fineness, her delicacy? If there had to be days when the world was flat for her in recompense there were the times when she was radiant and loving. And avid in bed.

What would Lydia say if she could see her delicate daughter tearing off her clothes, helping Lawrence with his, moaning with desire under him. She's a special kind of girl, he thought. Unique. Don't go on about it.

'Yes, that's true,' he nodded, smiling at Lydia because she looked concerned. 'People vary. Forget I mentioned it.'

He got into the habit, when they were all busy with the final preparations in the kitchen, of slipping out and going down the lane to the Wards' house. Mr. and Mrs. Ward were an affable colourless couple, but Judy, their daughter, had more character. She was a red-headed uncomplicated girl, he felt that she might be too straightforward at times, but that she was probably the injured party where her husband was concerned.

'Is my playmate ready to go tobogganing?' he would say. The little girl soon got to know him. 'Lawrie, Lawrie!' She jumped about while her mother wrapped her in warm layers of clothing, put furry mitts on her hands, furry boots on her feet.

He told himself he was a bit soft walking along the lane pulling Sue on a toboggan and wearing an idiotic smile, but he didn't care too much. When they got to the gentle slope of the field he would sit behind her, and with her safely cradled against his body, they would slide down to the hollow where the brook was frozen. Cuckoo Wood lay beyond. That was where it all started, he thought, and the name of the boy Julia spoke of came into his mind. Crawford North. It was like a cloud over the sun.

But the sound of Sue's laughter, and the sight of her rosy cheeks soon cheered him. Looking at her he would think that Julia had the same delicacy of skin, the same fine texture. It was amazing that a skin should be twenty-two years old and still look like a child's. Fragile Julia, the Julia he had promised to protect. The Julia whom Lydia and Grant would rather not discuss . . .

On Christmas Eve they walked over the fields to find the yule log which Lydia thought the occasion demanded. She wore her fur coat and her cheeks were as pink as Sue's had been. Once or twice they took hands and ran like children, once they fell and rolled in the snow, laughing, until he lay on her body and kissed her quiet. He told himself he was very happy.

That evening they had the carollers in for hot punch, and when they had gone they laid their presents at the base of the tree which Lydia and Julia had decorated.

Once, catching Grant's eye, he felt there was something contrived about the whole business, that Lydia had read somewhere in a book a chapter entitled 'How to Spend Christmas in the Country,' and had followed it like a recipe for mince pies. And he felt that Grant realised this, but like him, didn't mind going through the motions.

On the morning of Christmas Day they all went to church, and seeing that Grant left a crumpled note in the offertory plate, Lawrence did the same. He had never discussed religion with Julia. He himself subscibed to a kind of liberal humanism, but was susceptible to the Christmas story. He didn't mind paying lip homage. Julia looked entranced in church, her voice rang out clearly, she hung her head humbly.

We should know more about what each other thinks, he thought, as the vicar's words floated comfortably on the periphery of his consciousness. We never discuss any abstract ideas, I'm too busy hoping we're happy, I'm afraid . . . What was he afraid of?

And yet she read a lot, he had seen a book by Wittgenstein in her workroom, a book of poems by Blake. It was surely unusual for a young married woman to occupy her mind with a modern philosopher or a prophetic poet? He knew she wrote copiously in exercise books, but since his discovery on that day when he came home from Amsterdam, he kept his eyes studiously averted. No human being could hope to completely understand another human being, even in marriage. She was a gifted girl, she was different. Who else but a gifted girl would quote Blake at him? He remembered her leaning against his arm on their drive down to Dorset, murmuring . . . could he remember it?

'This from Great Eternity a mild and pleasant rest named Beulah, a soft Moony Universe, feminine, lovely, Pure mild & Gentle . . .'

He couldn't remember any more.

'I adore absolutely Blake,' she had said, 'I adore absolutely his "Songs of Innocence". They make me weep.'

'You are too tender-hearted, my love,' he had said. His taste was more stringent, more modern. His opinions were clear-cut, he would have enjoyed an intellectual argument. But Julia was guided solely by her emotions. She rarely reacted cerebrally.

In church, standing beside her and singing the Christmas hymn, he was astonished at the sweetness and clarity of her voice, so true in pitch. Everything that emanated from her body was beautiful, he thought, its own expression. And then he remembered the unkempt flat he had come home to, the filthy drip-plate beneath the burners, the state of the bedroom, her own odour. But he shook the memory away. This beautiful girl beside him singing Christmas hymns was the true Julia.

They had their Christmas dinner in the middle of the day because they were having a cocktail party at night. The dinner was too rich with its bread sauces, its brandy sauces, its cream, and made him feel sluggish. He would have preferred to have taken a long walk over the fields, but Lydia and Grant were resting, and Julia thought they should do the same. They didn't rest. As always, in bed, she excited him, and he made love to her with a burping stomach and a sour taste in his mouth.

But after a bath and a change of clothes they came downstairs at teatime to help Lydia with her final preparations. It was to be a big party, the Wards, of course, all the knowable village people. Judy had said she would get someone to sit with the children. Grant told him that Gerry Susskind and his brother and wife had been asked. Gerry was staying with them for Christmas.

But Gerry, who was the first to arrive, came alone. Leo had a cottage in Provence, and he and his wife had had to go there suddenly because they had word of some flooding which had ruined the sitting-room floor. A stream had burst its banks above the house.

Lawrence was left to speak to him while Lydia and Grant welcomed the other guests. Julia was in the kitchen. Presently she would circulate offering the luscious titbits which she had made after tea.

'I didn't think your brother was married,' he said.

'Oh, yes, very happily. His wife is much younger than he.'

'He came alone with you last time?'

'Yes, because Aline is French and she goes to this cottage in Provence for most of the summer. They have twin boys. Leo encourages her to do this. He thinks she needs to get away from the atmosphere of the place occasionally with the children. I think he was secretly rather glad of the contretemps about their house. He doesn't enjoy English Christmases, says they're too constipating and bucolic for his taste.'

'It must be rather disturbing to live on top of the job when it's a job like that.'

'Not to Leo, but to Aline a little, and she misses her family. He met her when he was on holiday in France. But you mustn't think that there are patients running around tearing their hair out. It's rather like a well-run hotel, or better still, a health farm.'

The room was beginning to fill up. The noise, although not deafening as yet, was a steady hum, soon it would be almost impossible to hear oneself speak. Most people went around hating cocktail parties while continuing to go to them. Was this why they made such a noise? Acting out their indignation at finding themselves there?

'Thanks for sending me the three chapters of the French book, Susskind,' he said. 'I expect you got my letter saying that I liked your translation. You've kept the medieval ambience which I particularly wanted.'

'Thank you. I'm glad it suited.'

'I'd like to use you. I said that in my letter too, and I've written to Parmentier.'

'It's a long book. The three chapters were a dummy run, but as I told you before, I always like to meet the author so that we can discuss his theme. I don't like translating blindly from chapter to chapter.'

'Well, I'm sure he'd welcome that too. He's quite prepared to accept our choice, although he did mention that his friend was disappointed. It's a mistake to mix business with pleasure.'

'I feel guilty.'

'Don't. Her English was too stilted, she hadn't a feeling for the language.'

'I'll go over as soon as you give me the all clear.'

'I should leave it until the end of January. I happen to know that Parmentier is in Africa writing the scenario for his last but one book, *Dead Leaves*. Then, when you've been and got under way I'll nip across and get Parmentier to sign on the dotted line. We'll probably publish in September if you think you could be ready.'

'Yes, of course. I'm a quick worker. I like to get it flowing and keep it up to the end.'

'Good. I might go over early Spring and take Julia.'

'How is your wife? As beautiful as ever?'

'Well, I'm not the one to say that.' He turned. Julia was at his side holding a tray of canapés. She was wearing a chiffon dress with wide sleeves which had slid back showing her white, childishly thin arms. 'Hello, Mr. Susskind,' she said, shyly. 'Would you like one?' She held out the tray.

'Thanks. Those look delicious. I was just asking your husband if you were still as beautiful and now I see you are.'

'Oh . . .' She shook her head. 'Hasn't your brother come with you? And his wife?'

'No, worse luck. They've had to go to Provence unexpectedly. They've left their au pair behind to look after me, so I'm all right.'

'You could stay here with us. I'm sure Mother would be delighted.'

'How kind. No thank you. I've enough to do at Ainswick.' Lawrence wondered if the au pair came high in his list. He was a good-looking man, if fleshy, his eyes were lively and brown in his dark face. 'I'll see Leo before I leave and tell him I've met you again and that you shone like a Christmas star.'

'You'll turn her head,' Lawrence smiled. 'Look, we're monopolising you. I'd like to introduce you to someone who's on her own this Christmas as well. In a way, that is.'

'Who, Lawrence?' Julia asked.

'Judy. Judy Thomson,' he said to Susskind, 'she's a divorcée. Two children. One of them, Sue, is my special pet.'

He raised his eyebrows at Julia. 'Are you planning a quiver-full?'

'Children? No. We're not in a hurry. Oh, there's Judy. Judy! Come and meet Mr. Susskind.'

Lawrence thought she was the kind of girl who should wear green. The vivid tone of her dress went well with her reddish hair. Also that if she came under Julia's scrutiny she might decide she was the classic English pear-shape. 'This is Mr. Susskind, Judy. Judy Ward. No, of course, it isn't Ward, that's your parents' name. Thomson.'

'The name of the man who ran away and left me.' She grinned without rancour.

'Men were deceivers ever,' Susskind said, 'but I'm the exception that proves the rule. My wife ran away and left *me*.'

'I'm sorry,' Judy said. 'Have you any children?'

'No.'

'Well, it's a relief in some ways. I've got two. Lawrence is in love with my Sue, aged three and a bit, aren't you, Lawrence?'

'Totally,' he said, smiling at her, thinking that it would be good if they got on well together.

Judy was talkative. Perhaps she had been drinking before she came. 'You know,' she said, smiling impartially, 'this girl Julia is as pure as the driven snow we see outside our window. She believes in the faithfulness of men. Someone should disillusion her.'

Lawrence laughed. 'I like her that way.'

'Well, of course,' she said, he could see that Judy was pulling his leg, 'it's in your own interest, isn't it? What do you think he does when he goes away on his business trips, Julia?'

'I don't know.' He remembered that she hadn't much sense of humour. He hoped Judy wouldn't go on too long.

'He jumps into bed with the first woman he meets, of course, or the nearest to hand. Isn't that so, Lawrence?'

'No,' he said, 'who would with a wife looking like Julia?'

'Who indeed?' Gerry said, raising his glass to Julia. She wasn't smiling. She looked round the three of them, Lawrence could see that her lip was trembling.

She stammered and then spoke quickly, 'Did you know that the house where Judy is staying is where my friend Crawford North used to live? It was his grandparents' house.'

Oh, God, Lawrence thought, oh, God . . .

She was obviously upset. She hesitated, then her voice came, like a brook tumbling over stones, 'Yes, he stayed there often when I was small. This was *my* grandparents' house, here, and so we played together a lot. We had all kinds of exciting games . . .'

'Like the kind I play with your Sue,' Lawrence looked quickly at Judy but not too quickly to miss the expression on her face. 'Do you know,' he smiled and put his arm round Julia's waist, 'do you know that Sue holds me in the hollow of her little hand? I think I'll wait until she grows up and then get rid of this girl.' He was conscious that Julia was shaking.

She smiled, looking calmer. 'I often thought I would

wait until Crawford North grew up and then we would get married. I used to dream about him . . .'

'And then I came along,' Lawrence said. 'Julia, darling, people are absolutely famished and you've made all those tiddly bits. Don't you think you should circulate?' He gave her a little push. Her eyes were strange, inward-looking. 'Julia,' he said again, 'wake up, circullate.'

She suddenly smiled at him. Her eyes were wide and clear. 'Circulate, oh, yes, I must circulate.'

Gerry Susskind was acute. He would notice the look of strain on Julia's face. So would Judy. He started to make some kind of explanatory remark and then saw that they were both deep in conversation with each other. He drew in his breath. They were sophisticated. Judy was putting on a good act of listening intently. Gerry was going through the motions of a male bent on charming the opposite sex.

And had he in any case been hyper-sensitive? Wouldn't they just take it as Julia, Julia who was unworldly, unconventional, who spoke her thoughts as they rose to the surface of her mind, who didn't sieve them first? But you couldn't discount the doubts. With someone else, Kate for instance, why was *she* always at the edge of his mind, there would be no doubts, anything she said would be completely acceptable while bearing the imprint of her own personality. Normal. He shied away from the word, caught sight of Colonel Luscombe who always came early and stayed late because he walked to and from his house. 'Good evening, Colonel. So nice to meet you again.'

'Look here, my boy,' Luscombe said, 'you're the one to explain it to me. Can you tell me what those fellows in Whitehall are up to?'

Lawrence didn't know, but he tried.

He and Julia had a long walk over the fields the next day. She was quiet, and looked pale. When they came to the Wards' house he suggested that they take Sue with them, but she shook her head. 'No, she might cry.'

'But she never cries. She loves being pulled on the toboggan.'

'She absolutely might cry and I can't stand children when they cry. They frighten me. Just be for me today, Lawrence,' she looked at him, her eyes wide and lost looking, 'just be for me.'

'I'm always for you,' he said. They walked through the snow, leaving virgin tracks on the fields, blue-white, but when he suggested that they should go as far as the Cuckoo Wood, she shook her head. 'It's too far away, Lawrence. I don't think I'll ever . . .' He stopped and put his arms around her. He felt her body shaking against his. 'What is it, my darling?' he said, his heart was wrung with pity for her.

But she wouldn't answer. When they retraced their steps the setting sun flooded blood red into their footprints.

The entire day they held open house to the followers of the hounds. They had met in the morning under a cedar weighted with snow which stood at the end of the lane. Lawrence had gone down to see them. He felt alienated from their kind of life, and Julia had said she couldn't bear to think of the poor fox. But there was a certain Christmas card rightness about the sight, the bright-clad figures moving around, the bodies of the hounds steaming in the frosty air.

Julia was bright and happy when the hunt came trooping in for sherries before they went off to bath and change for the dance that night. She moved amongst the men, chatting and laughing with them, and for once she seemed to respond to their open admiration.

'Let's go after all to the dance,' she pleaded with Lawrence.

'We agreed that we shouldn't go, that we were town mice.' But he gave in because she pleaded, and because it was hard to resist her radiant face. At the dance she was surrounded by red-faced youths bursting out of their stiff shirts. Lawrence, hovering on the fringe of them, heard their boasting about how the fox had been run to earth.

He teased her when they went into the buffet together. 'How about the poor fox now? I thought you were on his side. You seemed to listen with bated breath to the County's description of poor old Reynard's death rites.'

She looked at him without expression as if he had spoken a foreign language. He didn't exist for her. And he remembered that she had chosen fox fur for her new coat . . .

They went back to London the following day. Lydia and Grant were staying on until the end of the week.

He said to Grant when they were leaving, 'You and I have hardly had a minute to ourselves.'

'That's true enough,' Grant's handgrip was warm, 'but we might have talked business and then we'd have been in the dog house.'

Lydia said, kissing Lawrence, 'We've enjoyed having you. We've grown very fond of you.' He thought he saw tears in her eyes and wondered at them. 'Goodbye, darling,' she kissed Julia, 'Come and see us often when you get back. I miss you.'

'Oh, Mother!' Julia laughed, 'you'll be back on all your old committee meetings the minute you're home. You know you don't want me.'

'As long as you and Lawrence are happy.' Watching her Lawrence thought she looked strained, but then she'd had a busy time.

'Oh, we're happy all right,' he smiled at her.

'So we're all happy,' Grant said. 'Drive carefully. The roads will be slippy.' And then as an afterthought, 'By the way, Julia, do you ever drive now?' The remark couldn't have been more unfortunate.

'No, never,' she said shortly.

She didn't speak for a long time and he left her alone, thinking that one couldn't always guard one's tongue, but how some sixth sense had prevented him ever mentioning the car accident to Julia. Most people could take a fair amount of knocking, but not Julia. Definitely not Julia. At Winchester he put an arm round her and said, 'How's my Christmas girl?'

'Oh, Lawrence!' she said. When he put his hand back on the wheel she leant against him. 'Lawrence's Julia,' she said. Her sigh was a child's sigh, deep and shuddering, infinitely moving. It was his duty and his privilege, he thought, to love and protect her. The landscape looked flat and bleak. There was a bleakness inside him.

13

Julia got up from her chair and went over to the latest head which she had modelled. She looked at it critically for a long time, eyes narrowed. No, it wasn't any better. She had made the changes she had thought of earlier, the ears, the line under the chin, but somehow the eyes had gone wrong.

She saw where the mistake lay. She should have done a girl like Judy Thomson's Sue. Lawrence loved her, she was flesh and blood. How then could she expect him to like a clay head?

'It's no good, you know,' she spoke aloud in the quiet room, 'it's no good. You know what he wants.'

But I can't, she thought, wrapping her arms round her body, I can't, Lawrence, you have to look after me. It wouldn't do. You're too busy looking after me.

She felt cold. And sick disappointment. She went over to the electric fire and crouched down in front of it to get warm. She liked the play of heat on her face and body.

She gathered it into her, she felt restored. If she closed her eyes she could imagine she was back in Cuckoo Wood again. But she hadn't crouched like this, there. She had been straight and tall against Lawrence, heart to heart, she felt again the warmth which had flooded through her body at the contact. 'Lawrence,' she said aloud, 'help me...'

She went and sat at the table, opened the book she had been reading. She would write some of it down to steady her. This was a bad day and Lawrence wouldn't be in until late. He had told her that when he went away this morning. 'Go over and see Lydia in the afternoon,' he said, 'and I'll pick you up from there when I've finished with this boring dinner.'

'No,' she had said, 'there's a lot I have to do.' She had to keep up this pretence of a busy efficient wife, not a lost soul . . . So she must get busy. It was a waste of time with Lydia, lunching, meeting in Rest Rooms other women like Lydia, talking endlessly about new furniture and clothes and where to buy this and that and what to look out for, and how were the children . . . the children . . . she opened the book.

'Linguistic analysis,' she wrote. 'I can't understand this unless I find the way to use his language. Beyond the thinking there is . . . whereof one cannot speak thereof one must be silent. The poor fox was running and running through the wood, the Cuckoo Wood, Beulah, a soft Moony Universe. Reality is in death too, the world does not change but ceases. My child is dead. Lawrence does not love him. Ideas which do not operate are not part of reality reality reality . . . But Crawford North would take him. Lawrence, love me. Oh God what counts as death is not an event in life . . .'

She stopped writing and put her head in her hands. It was no good. This was a bad day. I'm sorry, Lawrence, sorry, sorry . . . She would give up writing. She would make a completely new head starting right from scratch and if she worked hard she could have it ready for him when he came home late tonight.

She felt purposeful. To have a purpose. Salvation. She got up and went to the clay bin and as she bent over it there was a ring at the doorbell. She ran downstairs feeling her light-heartedness in her feet. She flowed like a river . . . life was wonderful . . . she opened the door and Raymond was standing there with his anxious smile.

'Hello, Julia,' he said.

'Oh, hello, Raymond! I'm so glad to see you. Won't you come in?'

He shook his head, and she thought, he is the woman of the partnership, the mother, the harassed one, she remembered the bird she had lain in the ditch and watched, with the wisp of straw clinging to it, and its ruffled feathers . . . 'No, dear, sorry, I've just come to tell you that the janitor is ill. I went down to see him and he's got a shocking bout of bronchitis.' He shook his head and tut-tutted. 'He asked if you'd take your refuse down and leave it outside his flat where it'll be collected. He can't face the stairs today, poor soul. Would you like me to take yours? I've just been down with mine.'

'No, thanks, Raymond, I haven't much. I'll gather it together and take it down right away. I'm going to be busy . . . How's Roger?'

'Well, he's coming tonight, so I'm trying to get on with some typing work, five hundred envelopes to address. Still, it keeps the wolf from the door. Roger can't stay here but he helps with the rent. He says his father would flay the hide off him.'

'Would he? How sad. How's the epic going?'

'It's slow. I'm always being sent these awful typing jobs by the Agency, and although there's no brain fag I get awfully tired at nights. Sometimes Roger and I just sit around the fire and talk. He makes me laugh with his stories about his customers. He can mimic them a treat.'

'Is your ceiling all right now?'

'Oh, yes, dear. We got it done right away and Mr. Paton paid the bill. He was very decent. I hated to give it to him but he said not to worry. In fact, Julia, he gave us quite a bit extra. I wasn't going to tell you that.'

'I'm going to be very busy, Raymond, I've got a new idea for my head, you know the clay heads.'

'Yes, dear. Roger and I thought they were very nice.'

'You see, up to now I've always been doing a boy and now I see where I've gone wrong. It should have been a girl. I'm going to call her Sue when she's finished.'

'Oh, lovely, dear. Ask me in for a coffee sometime. I'd love to see it.'

'All right, Raymond, I'll do that. Sorry to rush away, and thanks for telling me about the dustbin.'

She ran into the kitchen. She took the plastic bag out of the bin, searched through her cupboards, found an empty Cornflakes packet and some paper bags, emptied the sink tidy into one of them. She put everything in the plastic bag and secured the top of it with a stout rubber band.

When she got to the outside door she remembered she hadn't brought her keys. It doesn't matter, she thought, I'll leave it open. It only takes five minutes to run downstairs. But when she was standing outside the basement flat she thought she ought to knock and ask Mr. Clewes how he felt. She could hear his shuffling feet, and then he was standing in the open doorway, grey-faced.

She smiled at him. 'Just to tell you my dustbin is here, Mr. Clewes. I'm sorry to hear you're ill. Can I bring you anything?'

'It's me tubes, miss. I'm dosing myself with a bottle I get at Boots.'

'I'll make you some hot lemon and honey,' she said, 'there's nothing better.' She felt full of life and compassion, a great lightness in her heart. Mr. Clewes was a grey, miserable man, grey-jerseyed, grey-scarved, she would like to help him in some way.

'Thank you, miss. It's not everybody that would bother. If all the tenants were as kind as you are I wouldn't have no cause for complaint, though I must say Mr. Mills is very good too. You can say what you like about him but I speak as as I find. Drat it!' He drew back as a black shadow streaked past him, 'That's Tommy away again. I can't seem to keep him in.'

She ran upstairs, went into the kitchen and squeezed two lemons, put the juice in a jug with three tablespoons of honey, filled the kettle, and when the water was boiling poured it into the jug. She was full of energy and desperate to get started on the new head. Holding herself up like this gave an exciting edge to her impatience. She could have a good day's work and she might even have it roughly finished by the time Lawrence got home.

She went downstairs again and gave Mr. Clewes the jug when he opened the door. 'Watch your hands, Mr. Clewes. It's very hot. I'm sure it will do you good.'

'Thanks, miss,' he said, 'you're a real lady.'

It gave her a nice feeling, bountiful, the right kind of feeling to begin on the head of Sue. She could hardly wait to get upstairs again to get started . . .

It was about three o'clock before she could bring herself to stop, but she had suddenly become intensely hungry. She knew only too well that she might lose her impetus, but her back was stiff and she felt a little dizzy because of her intense concentration. She mustn't get ill. Lawrence worried if she looked ill or pale. 'My Dresden piece,' that was another of his names for her.

When she went into the sitting-room with a cup of coffee in her hand and a plate with biscuits and cheese on it, she saw that some books had fallen from the bookcase and lay scattered on the floor. There were no spaces between the books, and so she thought they must have been resting on the top. She was only mildly anxious. Some chance wind, perhaps when she had banged the outside door . . . she kept thinking of the head upstairs, holding the idea in her mind. Halfway through drinking the coffee she put the cup down and went upstairs again.

But the earlier elation had gone. The head looked lumpy, lifeless, she hadn't caught the essential difference between a girl and a boy, a fineness, she had been so sure she knew where the difference lay. It was too disappointing. If she had kept going all day she would have had the head nearly finished to show Lawrence. 'Look, Lawrence,' she would have said, 'here is your little girl.'

She remembered that she hadn't finished her coffee and had forgotten to eat the biscuits and cheese. That had been silly. Lawrence often told her that she was to be sure and eat when he was away. She had promised faithfully.

When she went into the sitting-room she found one of a pair of bookends, a prancing Grecian horse, lying shattered on the floor. A curtain was pulled so that it hung awry half across the window. Now she remembered that she had thought she had heard a noise, and dismissed the idea, too busy to dwell on it.

Fear rushed into her suddenly. She sat down because she was shaking and when she put her hands to her face it was cold. There had been the books on the floor the last time . . . her heart hammered, making her feel sick, and she whispered, 'What is it?' afraid to look around. Because there was some kind of presence in the room, a watching, breathing presence. Could her heart be heard? She sat stiff with terror and then when she couldn't bear it any longer she got up and switched the central light on, then the table lamp.

Immediately she felt better. The room looked innocently familiar, in a minute she would find a reasonable explanation for the books and the curtain. But there was the horse. She had almost persuaded herself that she was imagining things but there was the plaster horse lying on the carpet with its head a foot or two away. She strove to keep her calmness, and her sanity. Once the window-cleaner had knocked over an ornament by banging, but he hadn't been today. He couldn't have come without her knowing. She had to let him in. But something like *that*. A reasonable explanation. There must be a reasonable explanation. She would go upstairs again, leaving the lights blazing in the kitchen, and the sitting-room, in the long narrow hall, on the stairs up to the attic. She hummed going upstairs, a tuneless humming.

But it was no use now. No use. She looked at her watch. Quarter to six. She had a gnawing sense of hunger, but worse than that a gnawing fear. But she wasn't petrified now, as she had been. Because Lawrence would soon be home. She would throw herself into his arms, say, 'Lawrence, there's something in the sitting-room, something evil, something waiting for me . . .'

She forced herself to work for ten more minutes but it was no good. Her hands were clumsy and trembling, she had ruined the girl's face, missing completely the infantile protrusion, the deeply-set eyes, missing completely the sex, it was a travesty of a face, it looked ugly, as evil as the something which was in the house, dark and evil. Lawrence, Lawrence . . . she crossed the room and crouched in front of the fire, hugging her body, come quickly, come quickly . . . and then she remembered. He had gone to a dinner, it would be at least ten before he would be home.

She lost herself completely, the girl crouched in front of the fire was an empty shell, a husk. She was playing in the garden with Crawford North. He was pushing her on the swing, higher and higher. 'Higher!' she screamed, 'if you push me higher I'll be able to see over the cedar, higher, higher . . .' and then she was no longer on the swing, she was crouched in the ditch and she had rolled over to see him above her. . .

She came back into herself trembling, there was some saliva running out of the side of her mouth. 'Silly girl,' she reproved herself, wiping her lips with a handkerchief, 'silly, silly girl. You can see it now. You've been concentrating too hard and you've tired your brain. You've been imagining things. Be sensible. Go downstairs into the sitting-room, have a whisky and soda, calm yourself. Then go into the kitchen and make yourself an omelette and open a bottle of wine. Lawrence encourages you to do this, you know he does.'

At the foot of the stairs a black shadow slipped across her feet and then seemed to double back towards the sitting-room. She stood, swallowing, her mouth dry with fear. She felt a scream tearing her mouth open, and yet there was the nightmare sensation that it was soundless. She tried again, but this time the scream was puny, dying in her throat.

There was something in the house. She would have to open the door and let it out, go and tell Raymond, tell anyone. She stumbled towards the door, dragged it open, got outside, breathing the different air of the hall as if it were ozone.

She seemed to have been watching this girl running for hours, hours upon hours. First she had knocked wildly at Raymond's door but there was no answer. Raymond and Roger must be busy. Then she had ran downstairs to Mr. Clewes' flat, but didn't knock there because she remembered as her hand was lifted that he had told her he would go to bed with the lemon drink and sweat it out.

Who, then? Richard? No, Richard might be at his surgery, in any case Richard looked at her with wise eyes saying nothing, she didn't like that look. Kate . . . her flat was quite near, two corners and then take the next turning on the right.

People seemed to be watching this girl running. She saw a man touch her arm and saw her shake him off. The girl caught sight of white faces, staring eyes, raucous voices shouting louder than the traffic, 'STOP, STOP . . .'

Here was where she had to turn. Ninety-one, wasn't

it? This was . . . this was . . . get your breath. Aaah . . .
eighty-five, odd numbers on one side, even on the other.
Thank God she was on the right side, eighty-seven,
eighty-nine, ninety-one, stumble up the steps, read the
cards, 'Miss Kate Henderson'. Push the swing door.

Nice staircase with red carpet, the still running girl
tripped on the carpet, bruised her knees, got up, ran on
upstairs. The carpet was too soft. Her feet sunk into it,
she had to pull her feet out of it, it was like a swamp trying
to suck her down.

First floor. 'Mr. V. Carter', 'Mr. P. Roland'. No, it's
the next one, the girl was getting tired, she stumbled
again, her hair was getting in her eyes. It should have
been cut long ago like Kate's, whirled on top of her head,
then people could see what she was thinking.

Here she was again. Heart thumping. 'Mr. Webster',
'Miss Kate Henderson'. Funny, the girl didn't remember
that that was Kate's name, but it should be all right. She
fell against the door, mumbling, mumbling, beating with
her hands, putting her face against the dark wood, seeing
the *trompe l'œil* graining, thinking, even in her agony,
that it was in bad taste. . . .

When Kate opened the door she saw Julia. Her hair
was wild, her face distorted, she was weeping bitterly.
'Kate, Kate,' she said, her voice wrung Kate's heart,
'there's something in our flat. Something evil . . . Kate,
you were the only one . . .'

'Come in, Julia,' she said, 'come in, darling. There's no
more need to worry. Come in and we'll have a cup of
coffee together and you can tell me all about it. I was
just making some.' All the time she was speaking she was
helping Julia into the hall, her arm round the girl's
shaking shoulders.

Lawrence was just in when the telephone rang. He hadn't
even had time to look around for Julia. She would

probably be in bed, he had decided. He had had a single moment of gut-twisting fear when he had seen the disorder in the sitting-room, but he had calmed himself. Take it easy, there must be a perfectly good explanation. Take it easy.

It was Kate. 'Lawrence, I've tried you several times. I couldn't get hold of you.'

'I was at a publisher's dinner.'

'Oh, that's it. It was too late to phone the office to find out.'

'What's wrong, Kate?'

'Don't get too worried. I've got Julia here.'

'Julia!' His skin crawled. 'Is there something wrong?'

'No, it's all right now. Richard has been. He's given her a sedative. He says she's to sleep here tonight and you can come and take her home tomorrow morning. He'll pop in early before his surgery to see how she is.'

'What's wrong?'

'We don't know yet. She arrived here in a state of terror saying there was something in the room. We can't make sense out of it, thought that perhaps it was her imagination...'

She was still talking, but he hardly heard. His senses were alerted, his ears pricked. There *was* something in the room, the faintest of movements, and surely there was a putrid smell? He wasn't imaginative, but by God there was something here, and the scrape of noise was coming from behind the radiator at the window. 'Hold on, Kate,' he spoke sharply.

The radiator was about a foot from the wall. He went over and peered down behind it, feeling foolish and yet uneasy. His mouth was set, he was taut with apprehension. Only darkness, as he had expected, but wasn't there a darker darkness, and two points of light? A movement? And then it dawned on him and he felt his face suddenly cold with sweat. A cat! Poor Julia. Somehow it had got into the house without her knowing. It had been mad to get out, had jumped on surfaces, probably thrown itself against the window . . . he looked down at the slivers of paint, saw the books on the floor, and then the broken plaster horse.

He went back to the telephone. 'Kate, are you there? I've solved the mystery. I'll ring you back in five minutes.'

He hung up the receiver and went into the hall. His nerve had returned, but, poor Julia! She must have been petrified with fear. A walking-stick would do. It would probably be fierce because of its terror, he wouldn't like to have it fly at him if he attempted to lift it. He opened wide the outside door, went back to the radiator and poked gingerly with the stick, trying to put it behind the darker darkness. 'Puss, puss,' he said encouragingly. 'Come on, then. Out you come.'

There was a hiss and then he saw it, large and black, streaking for the door. He followed quickly and saw it hurtling down the stairs. He remembered now that Old Clewes had a black tom, a lady-killer. It had come the wrong way. Poor Julia!

He went back to the sitting-room, poured himself out a stiff whisky and with it in his hand dialled Kate's number.

'Kate, it was a cat, a dirty great tom behind the radiator. We need all the perfumes of Arabia here now. Julia must have been scared out of her wits. There are books and things scattered about. It must have gone berserk because it found itself trapped.'

'Oh, poor Julia,' she said, 'she could have done without that.'

'I'll come round right away.'

'I don't think she'll waken.'

'I'll come round anyhow, if you don't mind. I'll open the windows and spray some of Julia's perfume about. I'll be there in five minutes.'

Kate opened the door to him. 'What a business!' Her expression was rueful.

146

'Yes, anyone else . . . anyhow, thanks for your help.'

'I did nothing. I would have done anything to have spared her this. Come in.' The last time I was in this bedroom, he thought, things were different. Very different. It seemed like years ago.

They both stood looking at the sleeping girl. Her hair had been brushed smooth by Kate and coiled neatly on top of her head. Worn like that the full beauty of her face was apparent, the indestructible bone formation. She was pale, her eyes looked bruised underneath. Occasionally, in her sleep, she gave a long, shuddering sigh.

'My poor darling,' he said. His heart overflowed with compassion for her. He bent and put the back of his hand against her cheek. His whole body yearned to comfort her, this unfortunate one who found life so difficult, who tried so hard, who found countless obstructions in her path over which she stumbled and fell. Would it always be like this? Would time give her her maturity, courage to bash out at life, to withstand the normal tensions of life? Did a trapped, smelly old cat come under that heading? Only if you had a sense of humour, perhaps. He bent and kissed her pale cheek.

When he straightened, his eyes met Kate's. There was pity in them, and as they looked at each other he knew, standing by the bedside of his wife, that it was Kate whom he loved but that it was Julia who needed him. Who would always need him. 'Kate,' he had to relieve his aching heart, 'Kate . . .'

'Come and have a cup of coffee,' she said.

They didn't speak much. Once he stretched out his hand and she grasped it in hers, her eyes quizzical. 'Hello, there.'

'Hello. I'm not a cheerful chappie. Sorry.'

She made it easy for him by talking. 'I'll bring her round to your flat tomorrow morning before I go to work. Richard will see her first.'

'Thanks. I'll either stay off work for a day or take her to her mother's. We'll see what she's like.'

'Yes,' she said, 'but I'm sure she'll be all right.'

'You see, Kate,' they were drinking the strong black coffee which she had made, 'it would frighten anyone, something like that. Even I jumped a bit at the beginning. It's so . . . bizarre! Julia is highly-strung, I've talked to Richard about it, but an incident like this, you couldn't blame her for being upset.'

'Of course not.' She turned away her head.

'You see, Kate, it's not her fault, you and Richard might have said, that's Julia again, getting upset over a trifle, which I admit she does sometimes . . . there was that time I came home from Amsterdam and she was lying in bed . . .' He bit back the words, apathetic, dirty . . .

'You don't have to talk about it.'

'No, I *know*,' he had an intense wish to vindicate her in Kate's eyes, 'but don't you see she always has *reasons* . . . she's sensitive, feels more intensely, well you've only to see the work she does with that clay. You've seen it yourself. Richard says that marriage can be upsetting for someone of delicate sensibilities. I suppose the concept of two people living closely together is difficult for some people who have lived a solitary life. The Amsterdam thing, Kate. She's a very loving girl, she has to give love, to receive love, she needs constant reassurance because she's not sure of me yet. But you see she had a reason then just as she has a reason *now*. I mean, what would you have done if you had found a cat in your room?'

She thought his voice lacked assurance. Probably what you did, poked it out with a stick. . . . 'I'm sure I should have been just as upset as Julia.'

'So you see, you can't say she's . . . she's unbalanced in any way, can you? Think of the shock and being alone in the house, and . . .'

He talked on, trying to pour salve on his soul and she

let him. But he knew that if their eyes met she would see
fear in them, and he would have to throw himself on her
breast and ask for her love. He gradually stopped
talking and looked silently at his cup for a long time.
Then he got up and said he must go.

The following morning Kate brought her home as she
had said. Richard had rung him when the two girls had
left and said that she seemed all right, but he would like
to have a chat with Lawrence. Could he look in on his
way home? It would be better than Richard coming to
their flat.

She looked a little pale and shaken, but she was perfectly normal. 'Oh, Lawrence!' She flung herself into his
arms. 'I absolutely was frightened out of my skin. I don't
know what Kate must have thought of me. Wasn't it a
dreadful thing to happen?'

'Yes, darling. Now I'm going to take you over to your
mother's for today, and then I'll fetch you at night.' He
had decided that there was no point to be gained in
treating her as an invalid and Richard had concurred
with this. 'Don't step out of your routine,' he had said,
'but see that she has company for today.'

'All right,' he was surprised she was amenable, 'I don't
want to be in the house alone. Will you be sure to come
for me in the evening?'

'Try and stop me.'

'I'll be going,' Kate said. She didn't look at Lawrence.

'Thank you a thousand times, Kate, dear.' Julia got up
and timidly kissed her on the cheek. 'There,' she said, 'I
haven't dared do that before, but Kate was so good to me,
Lawrence, honestly, so good to me.'

'It was nice to have you to look after,' Kate said.
'Come any time. But not so precipately.' She smiled. She
was playing the incident down. He was grateful to her.

'Right,' he said, trying for breeziness, 'we'll just lock up
here and then we'll deliver you to your mother. I've

phoned her. So you have nothing absolutely to worry about.' He smiled, teasing her.

'I'm not so worried,' Julia said, 'but you're both so good to me, so good . . .' she looked from one to the other, 'so good and kind, the two of you, I don't deserve it . . .' Her eyes for a moment looked full of comprehension, mature.

'Nonsense and chin-chin,' Kate said. 'Can't stand here gassing all morning.'

He played the incident down with Lydia as well. 'One adorable daughter who got a fright from a mangy old cat. She'll tell you about it. I'm going to take her to Paris soon to make up for it.'

'Are you, Lawrence?' Her face was calm, she showed no excitement. 'Mother, I'm just going upstairs to get a hanky. I forgot one.'

'There are plenty in your room.'

'Tell me, Lawrence,' Lydia said when they had heard Julia's feet on the upstairs hall, 'what's this all about?'

'Just a nuisance of a thing. She was alone at the time and when she discovered the cat she streaked round to Kate's. Richard has seen her. I'm going to have a talk with him later. Just keep her happy for today.'

'Of course. What a pity! She's never been very fond of animals. She didn't want pets when she was small either . . .' She stopped speaking and he thought her eyes were guarded.

He decided suddenly. 'By the way, it's nothing, really, just curiosity, but Julia seems to have an obsession about this boy, Crawford North, who lived in the house the Wards have now.'

'Crawford North?' She looked blank, then nodded. 'I know now, he was the grandson of the Carringtons who lived there, their daughter's son. For a moment the name didn't mean anything to me.'

He had seen the look before.

'They seemed to have been pretty good friends. She talks about him quite a lot.'

'I wouldn't have said so. Julia was a very shy little girl. We all thought they would have been good playmates, but we couldn't get her to go near him.'

'Oh,' he said. He was shocked and baffled. There was the nagging indecision again, the feeling of trying to find his way in a fog.

'Did you ever find her . . . making up things when she was small?'

'Well,' she laughed, 'what child doesn't?'

'What child doesn't.' He repeated the words. But that was the point. She was no longer a child. And that brought him back to what he had read in the open exercise book last night before he had gone to bed. And again at three o'clock when he couldn't sleep. 'Must dash,' he said. 'See you tonight.'

The fear stayed with him as he drove through the morning traffic, all day as he dealt with one business matter after another, was increased when he called in to see Richard. Richard was terse, a medical man today rather than a friend. He admitted that he was worried about Julia, but that he didn't trust his own judgement, and would Lawrence consider taking her to see Leo Susskind. There was none better.

'Was she in a state when she got to Kate's?'

'Yes, a bit of one.'

They both agreed that it would be fraught with difficulty if the visit to Leo Susskind was suggested at this stage, and that it would be better if a reasonable excuse could be found for going down to Dorset.

'Something to do with the cottage,' Lawrence said, 'I'll think something up.' Richard would call in now and then to see her until the visit was arranged. He would keep an eye on her.

But the fear was there again as he drove up the long drive to the Fairfields' house, it stayed through the pleasant dinner which Lydia had prepared for them and at which Grant was his charming self, Lydia was cool and capable, and he, Lawrence, provided the light relief. It was a game of charades. Once between the courses Julia rested her chin on her hand and her neck drooped.

'Tired?' he asked her.

She nodded.

'Wait till I take you that weekend to Paris. You'll have the time of your life.'

She smiled at him sadly, humouring him. His heart filled.

14

But, as it happened, the excuse was presented to him the next morning by Grant. He had rung through on the inter-office telephone and asked Lawrence to come and see him.

'Sit down, Lawrence,' he said when he appeared, 'this may take some time. I didn't want to upset Julia further by any discussions in her presence. That was an unfortunate experience with the cat.'

'Yes, it was. With anyone else it might not have mattered . . .' He decided to take Grant into his confidence. 'I'm worried about her. I saw our doctor last night and so was he. He wants her to see Leo Susskind.'

'The psychiatrist?'

'Yes.'

There was a pause. Grant played with the pencil in his hand, then, as if coming to some decision, he tapped it once on the desk. 'I'm as worried as you are, surprised too. But perhaps not as completely surprised. It doesn't confirm what I was thinking, rather what I *wasn't* thinking, what perhaps Lydia and I have never faced up to. Don't imagine I'm going to reveal some dreadful skeleton in the cupboard, but for a long time we haven't given voice to our worry, only known that it was there. We knew she was different, that was all, hoped, like many parents, that it was growing pains.'

'In what way different?'

'I can't pin it down. Just that she was, her reactions were different, she was anti-social, unlike girls of her own age. Well, shyness is a common girlish complaint, especially for an only child. Then she hadn't many boy-friends, to be quite frank, she hadn't any. We used to wonder if her looks scared them off.'

'Did you ever take her to see a doctor?'

'Yes, I persuaded Lydia to do this. There was some female complaint too. But we have a fool of a man, at least he's good in his own field which is ministering to people with a good bank-book and trying to say what they want to hear. But I've suspected for a long time that he's not very up-to-date.'

'What did he say about her?'

'Just what we knew. That she was highly-strung, that she was going through a difficult phase, you know the thing. Lydia agreed with him. She thought I was too concerned, and I retracted, thinking after all that it was female territory. But I realise now Lydia agreed with him because she wanted to. She's by way of being a perfectionist, she could not conceive that a daughter of hers could be anything but a normal, fashionable young girl. You couldn't blame her.' He looked at Lawrence.

'No I suppose not.'

'So she was given the usual treatment. A tonic for anaemia, fashionable boarding school, fashionable finishing school, groomed this way and that. We indulged her wishes a little over the Art School but we tried to enforce our own too, for her own good. Lydia and I, I think, just kept our fingers crossed in the hope that it was, those tired old words, "a phase she was going through". How often have parents pinned their hopes on that one?'

'Richard Lewis, our doctor, thinks it may be more serious.'

'But she's happily married. She adores you. She looks happy.'

'He's still worried.'

There was a pause, and then Grant said, 'So am I. Did he say any more than that?'

'No, he wouldn't commit himself. Just that he would like her to see Leo Susskind without wasting much time.'

Grant looked miserable. He played with the pencil, his handsome face was stern in thought, and for the first time Lawrence saw signs of age in it, a portent of what he would look like as an old man, the downward mouth, the sagging muscles in the neck. 'Lawrence . . .' He looked up. 'I've got to say this although I'm deeply ashamed about it. As a matter of fact, Lydia and I had discussed whether we should say anything to you . . . well, we decided not to. Oh, it wasn't a great sin, just one of omission. And then we were her parents. Parents get the best but sometimes the worst out of their children. We thought we might have been handling her wrongly. But, in our defence, we genuinely felt that once she was married and there was a home to look after and possibly children she'd settle down.'

She doesn't want children. She's afraid of them.'

'Afraid to have them?'

'No, just afraid. She's terribly vulnerable. The whole concept of motherhood frightens her. She wants only to be protected by me. I think she sees herself quite plainly at times, her shortcomings, which are not really shortcomings as Richard has explained to me, but signs of an illness. She has a good intellect.' He looked down at the desk. 'I'm worried about those times . . .'

'You don't think she would do herself any harm?'

'How can one tell? How can one know the agony another soul goes through?'

'Lawrence, this is terrible.'

'I'm not trying to panic you. Only I feel you should know as much as I do, which isn't much.'

'I can't say how sorry I am.'

Sorry for Julia, or sorry he had withheld information? Sorry about the marriage? Lawrence spoke roughly, 'Don't feel sorry. I wanted to marry Julia, I fell in love with her. If you had told me anything about her I don't think it would have changed my decision in the least.' But it might have postponed it, and there had been Kate.

'Do you still love her?'

He saw Kate. He saw her in all her normality, fresh, loving, healthy, and for a moment the pain was so great that he didn't speak. 'Julia depends on me,' he said, 'I'll never let her down,' and then, seeing the doubt still in Grant's face, he lied, or was it a lie? 'I love her.' He wished suddenly that he had a religion behind him, the religion which taught that bad as things may be they will never be too dreadful to bear.

'Cheer up, Grant,' he said, and smiled, 'we may be being unnecessarily gloomy. The person to think about in this is Julia, nothing else is important. The thing that's exercising my mind at the moment is how I can persuade her to see Leo Susskind professionally without upsetting her or making her more fearful.'

'As it happens, I can give you an excuse. I should have told you this right away but my mind was full of Julia.'

'Well, let's hear it.'

'It's quite a long story. Have you time?'

'If it concerns me, yes. I've got an appointment at eleven-thirty.'

'Well, Gerry Susskind phoned me this morning. He tried to get you, actually, but you weren't in.'

'I stayed with Julia until I was sure she would be all all right. I'm not happy leaving her, but Richard will be looking in later on.'

'This is an amazing tale. You'll scarcely credit it.

Gerry, as arranged with you, I imagine, went over to Paris to see Parmentier. He says they got on like a house on fire and Parmentier was quite happy to have him do the translation.'

'Fine.'

'Just wait. He asked Gerry if he'd mind having dinner with this friend of his, Jacqueline...'

'That's the girl who wanted to do the translation?'

'Yes. He got the impression that Parmentier was using him as a shield...'

'Go on.'

'They went to a café in Montmartre. Jacqueline became objectionable and halfway through the meal she accused Gerry of stealing her job and made at him with a knife.'

'Good God!'

'Quite. Fortunately he had put up his hand to protect himself, and all he got was a bad gash on it. The proprietor came running in on the scene, divested Jacqueline of the knife, and it ended up with her sobbing in a heartbroken fashion... he said she was as drunk as a coot.'

'Or drugged.'

'Maybe.'

'Gerry said it was typically Montmartre. All it needed was a few Apache dancers!'

'He seems to have taken it well.'

'Yes, it couldn't have happened to a better person. Well, the proprietor was anxious that the good name of his café shouldn't be ruined if the *flics* were called in, and added his lamentations to that of the girl. So he said okay, he wouldn't prefer charges. I forgot to say that Parmentier, the only one apart from Gerry who seemed to have kept his head, had gone into the kitchen and brought back some clean cloths with which he bound up Gerry's hand. It was bleeding profusely all over the table by this time. Gerry said one of the tarts at a nearby table fainted. Parmentier then took Gerry right away to his own doctor who put three stitches in the hand and said it would be all right in a week or so.'

'He'd be as guilty as hell.'

'Yes.'

'But Gerry's not litigious?'

'Not a bit of it. He laughed it off on the telephone, said he was glad it wasn't his left ear, and that he was staying with Leo for a week or so because he was unable to type. I gather it's a second home to him.'

'I'll go and see him.'

'That's what I thought. And now that you say your doctor wants Julia to see Leo Susskind, you could make Gerry the excuse.'

'Yes . . . yes, you're quite right. I'll telephone him today.'

'Fix it up as soon as you can, and, Lawrence, take a week off until you see that Julia's all right.'

'Yes . . .' He felt obscurely annoyed that Grant should now rush him when he had been so secretive about Julia before. But, what could he have said? I've a daughter who is likely to develop a mental illness? 'Richard's got her under mild sedation,' he said.

'Drugs are wonderful nowadays. Psychology reduced to physiology. But take the time off.'

'All right.' He could understand Grant's insistence, his feeling of guilt. 'I've half-promised her a weekend in Paris. I was going to take the contract to Parmentier.'

'Well, there's all the more reason now and perhaps it would buck her up, a change of scene.'

'Perhaps.' He got up to go and then sat down again. 'Grant, since we're being pretty frank with each other, Richard asked me if there were any members of your family who had been, well,' he couldn't bring himself to use the word, 'unstable', 'well . . . unusual. He's been thinking about the hereditary factor.'

He thought Grant's face went white, but then it had

been a trying morning for any father. He didn't speak for a moment and then he said, 'Yes, there was. My sister.'

'What about her?'

'Julia's rather like her . . . She was a few years older than me and I didn't have much to do with her. I had been away from home at school and then university, and then I had married Lydia. No doubt my ageing parents found it convenient to have an unmarried daughter to look after them. At forty Esther met a man who had come to live in our village. He wasn't up to much. I met him once or twice. Retired tea-planter, boozy, opiniona-ted, a bit of a loud mouth. But we hadn't reckoned with the force of the desire which might afflict a forty-year-old spinster. She fell in love with him. Her first affair, can you imagine, at forty! He said later that she did all the running, plagued the life out of him, pitiable . . .' He looked at Lawrence.

Lawrence nodded, bit his lip.

'Well, to cut a long story short he used her. I can't believe there was much love on his side, but some men can't turn down a chance however unlikely. She became pregnant, which at forty is laughable if it weren't tragic, and she hid it from everyone. She must have gone through agony. When she was five months gone and pos-sibly frantic at the thought of the denouement, she took an overdose and killed herself. She left a note . . .' He stopped abruptly.

'What did it say?'

He held Lawrence's eyes. 'You'll never credit it. Just one sentence. "I didn't love him." '

Lawrence kept silent. He would tell Richard. Perhaps it had a bearing on Julia, perhaps not. He got up slowly. 'If Leo Susskind asks me about her background I shall have to tell him this.'

'Yes of course. God,' he said. 'Life's the limit, isn't it? All the wrong ones suffer.'

Lawrence nodded. He drummed shortly on the desk

with his knuckles, feeling embarrassed. 'Well, thanks, Grant . . .' He didn't know what to say. He closed the door behind him.

When he got back to his room he phoned Leo Susskind's house. It was a woman's voice who answered, young, foreign-sounding. 'Do you want Dr. Susskind or his brother?'

'Both, actually, if it's not too much trouble. Perhaps I might have a word with Dr. Susskind first.'

Leo knew him instantly, didn't waste words. 'Come down tomorrow,' he said when he had listened for a few minutes, 'the sooner the better. And don't spring it on her. Nobody likes to be tricked. Try and break the ice a little.'

'All right. It's kind of you to see her so soon.'

'Kindness isn't involved.'

'Will your brother be there?'

'Yes,' he laughed, 'we can't get rid of Gerry. Aline, that's my wife, spoils him, she's a true Frenchwoman. You heard about his spot of bother? I think she feels personally responsible!'

'Yes, I'm sorry about it. I'd like to see him.'

'Well, you can kill two birds with one stone. Come for lunch.'

'That's very . . . thanks, we'll do that.'

He left the office after lunch-time and went home. Julia was there, in the sitting-room. She was tidy, her hair was well-brushed, her trousers and sweater were clean. She had bare feet.

'Hello, darling,' he said, and kissed her. 'Not working today?'

'No, I'm experimenting.'

'Are you? What with?'

'Me. I haven't got over my fear of the cat so I decided to exorcise it. I've Hoovered and polished, and I've put a soapy cloth on a stick and poked it behind the radiator. I've rubbed and rubbed, Lawrence,' the face she raised to him was pale, 'but I can't get rid of the smell. It's all over the house. Everywhere I go.'

He sniffed loudly for her benefit. 'It's here a little. Not much, though.' He thought it better not to deny it completely. 'You've been very thorough.' He took his hand from behind his back. 'Perhaps these would help.' He had brought her a dozen red roses. 'I don't care about the colour,' he had said to the girl in the shop, 'I want some with a strong perfume.' The car had been filled with their scent.

'Why are you so absolutely good to me?'

'Because I absolutely love you.' He sat on the edge of her chair and put his arm round her. She put her head against his shoulder, not speaking. It was light against him. There's loving and loving, he thought, many kinds. The one I have for Kate is full, deep, rich, it would have been the basis for a happy home and children. But who do I think I am that things should go right for *me*?

'Julia, my darling,' he said, 'I'm going to take you out for dinner and then I'm having a few days off work.'

'Why? Not because of me?'

'Don't flatter yourself.' He hugged her shoulders. 'No, I've to go tomorrow to see Gerry Susskind. He's staying with his brother. He's had an accident to his hand.'

'What happened?'

'He got into a fight with a French author's former girlfriend. Since he was on firm's business, so to speak, I thought the only decent thing to do was to go and see him. You've been invited too.'

'I mustn't get in your way. Mother tells me that she made a life of her own once she saw how busy Father was. What do you make a life of your own with . . . ?' He thought he hadn't heard her properly. 'She says every married woman has to face up to this.'

'Well, you have. How about the bodiless wonders upstairs?'

'They won't come right. I was doing you a girl this time but it won't come right.' She started to weep, slow, bitter tears. He hadn't the heart to say that Leo Susskind wanted to see her.

15

She seemed better the next morning. Last night he had dried her tears and taken her out for a slap-up dinner, setting himself out like a clown to entertain her. Now he thought he was rewarded by an easy, normal Julia, one who looked forward to the outing to Dorchester almost with an innocent gaiety.

'Are you sure we won't be a nuisance to them going for lunch?' she asked in the car.

'No, of course not. His wife, Aline, is French. I expect she is a superb cook. And you've met Dr. Susskind before. At least you've seen him.'

'When was that?'

Too late he realised his mistake. 'Oh, long ago.'

'When, Lawrence?'

'That time I came down to Corfe Cottage before we were married and your mother had a cocktail party. When we went to Cuckoo Wood.'

'When I crashed the car?'

'You didn't crash it, at least, not deliberately, you skidded on some oil.'

'I crashed it. Was he the man who was standing beside you, a tall man?'

'Yes.'

They drove in silence. He hummed, feeling his own apprehension like a bad taste in his mouth. Suddenly he heard her laugh, high, mirthless, unlike herself.

'I know why you're taking me. It's no good hiding it.

You're taking me to see Dr. Susskind. He's a psychiatrist.'

'You're quite right.' He spoke calmly, but his heart was knocking against his ribs, 'I'm also going to see his brother. What I told you about him was perfectly true. But we've all been worried about you, you're too thin, you're always cold, you're easily upset, and now you've had another fright with that damned cat. You want to enjoy life, don't you?'

'Yes.' Her voice was dull.

'We can have such good times together. You're afraid to fly, afraid to drive, you can't go on being afraid, Julia. Dr. Susskind would like to help you.'

'Richard Lewis fixed this up, didn't he?'

'No, I fixed it. Richard suggested it. Julia, darling, let's see what comes out of it. He's clever, he's experienced, he's used to dealing with . . . girls like you.'

'You don't love me any more, isn't that it?'

'No, it isn't. I'll always love you.'

'But not the way you love Kate. I've known it for ages, the way she looks at you. The way you look at her. When you're like me you get very acute about other people's feelings. You can see right into their heads. Look at Raymond and Roger. I know you despise them, really . . .'

'I don't despise them.'

'Well you don't take them into account which is just as bad. I do. They're good and kind. They're my best friends.'

'You've got lots of friends, darling.'

'I used to have. They're all gone now. Kate could have been my best friend if you hadn't loved her.'

'You're imagining things. Kate cares for you deeply, as I do. All everybody wants is to see you well again. To please me, I don't often ask favours, do I, but to please me, let Dr. Susskind have a chat with you.'

She didn't reply. He drove on in silence, wondering how badly he had mishandled it, thinking he had done his best.

'All right,' she said suddenly, 'You know I'd do anything to please you. Julia's Lawrence . . . anything . . .'

They got to Ainswick just before lunch. They drove through the imposing gates flanked by what Julia called a gingerbread house. The drive curved between open expanses of lawn and flower beds, empty except for wallflower plants, and there was no dark bordering of trees. The pale winter sun gave the whole place a pleasant welcoming aspect, there was no feeling of being shut in. The house was Victorian Gothic, but dotted about the wide parkland there were little bungalows or chalets with red roofs.

When they stopped the car at the steps leading up to the house, two boys of about six, identically dressed in jeans and red jerseys, hurtled down them, followed at a more sober pace by an elderly spaniel who took the steps with sideways care.

'Hello,' they said as Lawrence got out of the car, 'Are you Mr. Paton?'

'Yes I am.' He smiled at them.

'Daddy told us you were coming. Is that your lady?' Julia had joined them.

'That's Mrs. Paton. Julia.'

She smiled nervously, and then seeing the old dog she said, 'He's nice. I like him.' She bent down and stroked the dog's soft ears, 'He's gentle.'

'He's a she,' one of the twins said. 'Her name is Crackers. I'm Jonty and that's Toby.'

'I'm three minutes older than he is,' Toby said.

'Jonty! Toby!' There was a girl at the door, dark, buxom, even at a distance she gave an air of capability. Lawrence took Julia's arm and they went up the steps towards her.

'It's Mr. and Mrs. Paton, isn't it?' She held out her hand. 'I'm Aline Susskind.'

'Lawrence and Julia,' Lawrence smiled, 'I hope we're not late.'

'Not at all. It's the cold lunch. Always I find this more suitable because Leo forgets to come in. So at night we have the big dinner when I know I have captured him for a time.' They were in the hall, now, pleasantly white-walled, a profusion of potted plants in groups on the floor and in jardinières, and she smiled at Julia. 'Come upstairs with me, please. May I call you Julia? Always it makes for better relationships, Leo says, but I can tell you in France we are much more formal.' She said to Lawrence, 'And you, Mr. Paton, Lawrence, perhaps you will enter the drawing-room.'

When he went into the room Gerry came forward to meet him. 'Well, this is nice,' he shook hands using his left one, 'What a *poseur* I am! It's completely better but I find I can get more sympathy this way. Relic of the *crime passionel*!' He waved his hand and laughed, 'Sit down. Leo is busy. He asked me to give you a drink. Dry or medium sherry?'

'Medium, please. Everybody scorns the poor medium because they think it's not in good taste.'

'I couldn't agree more. I like mine rich, dark and fruity.'

When they were both seated at the wide window looking on to the park, Lawrence said, 'I must offer my humblest apologies about the fracas in Paris. We feel partly to blame.'

'Forget it. It was an unavoidable incident, nothing more.'

'Thanks.' He decided to be frank. 'You know there's a double reason for my visit.'

'Yes. Let me reassure you, Leo is first-class. And just as important, he'll quickly win Julia's confidence. I remember her quite well. So beautiful. I should be hopeful if I were you.'

'You make me feel hopeful.'

Aline came into the room with Julia. She looked

164

relaxed. 'What a lovely house this is, Lawrence! Why don't we live in the country?'

'Because we've got to eat.'

'Hello, Julia.' Gerry got up and shook hands. 'Sit beside me and then you can enjoy the view. Now you know why they can't get rid of me.'

'Do they want to?'

'Ask Aline.'

Aline laughed, 'No, he's very useful with the children.'

Leo came into the room. He smiled all round but went first to Aline whom he kissed, 'Hello, darling. You've been holding the fort with Gerry?'

'Yes, always you are late. We expect that now, don't we, Gerry?'

'He'll be late for his own funeral.'

Aline got up. 'I shall ask to be excused and see that my table is ready for you.' She smiled at Julia and went out of the room.

He admired Leo for going straight to the point. 'I'll tell you what the plan of campaign is.' He accepted a sherry from his brother. 'After lunch you and I, Julia, will go into my study and have a chat. Your doctor has told me that you've been unwell recently. We want to try to get to the bottom of it. Will you allow me to try?'

Julia looked out of the window. Lawrence saw the deep flush on her pale cheeks.

'Don't worry about me discussing this openly,' Leo said, 'there's nothing shameful in feeling ill. It's a by-product of our modern civilisation. Don't you agree?'

She shrugged, keeping her head turned away.

'After we've had our talk Gerry would like to show you the grounds. You may meet some of the patients. He has a bridge four amongst them and also I think, a pretty good squash opponent. Right, Gerry?'

'I'm still looking for a snooker pal.' Gerry laughed.

'Will you come too?' Julia said, looking at Lawrence.

'No,' Leo smiled at her, 'you see, Lawrence is the one

165

who knows you best and so if there is anything you've forgotten to tell me he can fill in the gaps. He has your welfare at heart, Julia, as we all have.'

She looked from him to Lawrence. Lawrence smiled at her, his eyes speaking, it's all right, don't worry. She looked hunted.

'Well, there it is,' Leo shrugged, 'I'm a dreadful person for organising. Aline will provide us with a sumptuous but fattening tea after all the talking, and then you'll be able to leave and be in London before bed-time.'

'We're hoping to go to Paris at the weekend,' Lawrence said.

'Paris? Well, some people have all the luck. Although *you* didn't, Gerry?' Leo laughed across at his brother.

'Well, you can't say I don't see life.'

Aline came into the room. 'Lucheon is ready,' she said, 'Come along, Julia,' she linked arms with her as Julia rose, 'You and I will lead the way.' Such kindness, Lawrence thought, the world is full of kindness . . . now you're getting maudlin on your fruity sherry.

'What worried you first about your wife, Lawrence,' Leo asked him. They were seated in his study. The lunch had been interesting because of the selection of pâtés made by Aline. Immediately afterwards Julia had been led away by Leo, and Lawrence and Gerry had sat in the drawing-room. By mutual consent the subject of Julia hadn't been raised, but they had slipped into an easy familiarity, discussing methods of writing, the world of books and the small change of that world, especially publishing.

What worried him first? Had it been tangible? He thought back, right back to their first meeting at her twenty-first party, then his weekend at Corfe Cottage. 'Vague stirrings,' he said, 'a feeling of strangeness, nothing much.'

'The incident about the car? Remember I was at the cocktail party her parents gave. She skidded.'

'Yes, she skidded.'

He thought hard, one should keep a diary, and then he remembered the day when they had come home from their honeymoon and she had seen the vase of flowers. 'A vase,' he said, 'a white vase. She went on about it. It puzzled me at the time.'

'She found it significant?'

'Yes. How did you know that was the word she used? She asked me that, I remember. "Didn't I find it significant?"'

'People like Julia are searching constantly. They can imbue ordinary objects with a special meaning, the sight of a vase, or a chair, could suddenly burst upon them as if it held the meaning of the universe. Did you worry a lot about this? Did it strike you as strange at the time?'

'No, not really. I'd got the hang of her, so to speak, or thought I had. I told myself that I loved her more because she was different, unusual. I was rather proud of her "exquisite sensibilities", as the novelists call it.' It was coming back to him now, the aura, the ambience she created, 'I think the next thing was the heads.'

'The heads?'

'Yes, she spent a lot of time up in her workroom, an attic above our flat. She models in clay, you know, there must be about fifteen or twenty heads up there. It was before I went to Amsterdam...'

'Was that a business trip?'

'Yes.'

'Were you going alone?'

'Ostensibly. Actually I was going for the purpose of bolstering up our Foreign Sales editor.'

'A man?'

'No, a woman. Kate. She's a friend of both of us. I knew Kate before I knew Julia, but Julia liked her...' he turned away his head as he spoke. This Guru sitting there would be asking him about Kate next, and then he thought, that's unfair, he's reasonable, he's clever, he's going to do his best for us . . . 'It was just a short visit to Amsterdam, one or two nights, but before I went Julia asked me to come up to her workroom and gave me one of her heads, a head of a child.'

'Did she say anything?'

'Yes, I can remember that . . .' his voice stumbled. ' "It's . . . it's for you," ' she said, "I made it for you . . ." ' There was a shining bright light in his brain. He had known it all the time, had not brought it to the surface, giving me a child before I went off with Kate . . . that was it. 'The next time,' he nodded at Leo, 'I don't have to think now, the pattern emerges, was when I got back and she was in bed, dirty, unwashed . . .'

'That shook you?'

'Yes, that shook me. But again there were extenuating circumstances. I had been delayed by a day. If she had been worried about me with Kate . . . and then Richard said that newly married girls could be sensitive, especially someone like Julia.'

'And you accepted this?'

'Partially. But I think it was around this time that I began to get really worried about her. She was too solitary, too thin, always cold. She worked upstairs alone for long hours during the day, she read a lot, and she wrote . . .'

'What did she write?'

'Extracts from poems, that sort of thing, Blake . . . I read them. They were a bit . . . garbled.'

'Word salads. Distressing for you, but revealing. Funny how everybody finds themselves in Blake. Some like him for his obscurity and violence, Julia probably for his gentleness. She's gentle most of the time, is she?'

'Yes, gentle and kind. Underneath it all . . . Well, I think the next thing was the cat.'

'Tell me about the cat.' Lawrence felt he knew already, but told him in detail nevertheless, finishing by saying, 'She ran out of the house.'

'Who did she go to?'

'To Kate. The girl I was at Amsterdam with, I mean, the girl who was at Amsterdam . . .'

There was a pause. This too must be significant. He hated Freudian symbols if that was what it was. He remembered seeing a button in a Carnaby Street Shop window, 'Freud is finished.' He had nearly bought it for a joke.

'To Kate.' Leo looked at Lawrence. I've never seen a Jew with happy eyes, he thought, they must be born sad.

'Richard is a friend of Kate's, and she called him to her flat, that's how he came in on it. Of course he's our doctor too. I gather he must have seen her when she was pretty distressed. He sedated her. Well, you know the rest. He thought she should be investigated.'

'I feel I've been hammering at you, Lawrence, all questions and no explanations.'

'Do you mean you don't know what's wrong with her?'

'No. It's pretty clear-cut, but you can help me to fill in the picture. You're at the receiving end and fairly normal, I should think. Think carefully. Have you ever noticed a random change of direction in thought, a sudden blocking and then off in another direction. There's an apt phrase for it, "Knight's move".'

'You mean a kind of zigzag approach?'

'Yes.'

'I may have done. But I should think that might apply to anyone from time to time. We're all a bit mad.' He went brick red.

'That's true enough.' Leo was looking at his pen, rolling it between his fingers. 'Have you ever felt that you had a complete lack of rapport with Julia, absolutely no human empathy, when something she was doing or saying seemed so bizarre that you questioned your *own* sanity? Take your time.'

He did. But it was no good. Everything he had told Leo had had a reason, an extenuating circumstance behind it. He admitted to unease, fear, sometimes, he was feeling it now, there was the stupefaction of reading that stuff in her notebooks, but then Leo hadn't made much of that, and it could be called simply a kind of mental doodling. 'No,' he said, 'I was terribly afraid when I read the last stuff, a hash-up of Wittgenstein, I was deeply disturbed . . .'

'So was she when she wrote it. There's this search you see for explanations . . .' He looked up at Lawrence, 'But there has never been complete lack of rapport?'

'No.' And then he added, 'You see, I love her.' Love, pity, in any case he was responsible for her.

Leo had been reading his mind. 'You're right to think there were extenuating circumstances in the various incidents you've told me about. But of course we must bear in mind that everyone has to face incidents, they're the very stuff of life. It's not circumstances which are important, it's one's reactions to them. But, yes, I give you your point. However . . . if the situation worsens, if the time comes when there is some kind of florid display . . .' He smiled at Lawrence. 'I've tried hard not to use any medical jargon. I always feel it's an admission of failure to communicate on the part of the physician. Where was I? Oh, yes, if you feel, out of a clear blue sky, that your link with her is completely gone, that there is a . . . a glass wall between you, then she must come here for treatment. I've given in to her on this point for the moment. She begged me not to take her away from you, and, of course, I'll be in touch with Richard to put her on medication right away. In many ways she would be better under my care so that I could watch her reaction and response to drugs, but we'll see how it goes.'

'Poor Julia.'

'I ask you not to feel too badly about it. In an extreme state of distress she would be so far removed from you that she would feel no sorrow about leaving you. And the other point is that a manifestation which leaves you in no doubt is almost a good thing. It's rather like a boil when it's ready to burst. Drastic states need drastic remedies. So be hopeful, and should she worsen suddenly, don't despair. Remember that old saying that you've got to get worse before you get better.'

'Is there a cure?'

'What is a cure? There might well be.'

'It isn't a brain tumour or anything like that?'

'No, nothing like that. She's schizophrenic. The least I can promise you is a partial adjustment, the best that you'll live happily together for many years to come.'

'Am I essential to her adjustment?'

'I should say you're essential.'

'And how about a family?' He regretted that.

'It's important to you?'

He shrugged. 'Forget it.'

'Ask me again in a year. But you'll have a role to play, an important one. I should say your life-style has been fixed for you, Lawrence, as far as Julia is concerned. You're not a fool. You must recognise this. But I don't think you'll sell yourself short. You've a positive attitude to life, the normal one, facing up to a problem and dealing with it as far as you can, going on to the next one. Yes, I should say you're absolutely essential to Julia.'

'She trusts me?'

'She depends on you. Utterly. It's hard.' His eyes probed into Lawrence. 'Only you know how hard, eh? I can give you no consolation except to say that there's no conceivable human condition in which you can be relieved of the tension between what you have done and what you ought to do. Man is ultimately self-determining. So there's no escape, at least no escape for anyone who has a conscience.' He smiled. 'I'm not giving you much comfort.'

'No, but perhaps courage, which I greatly need.' Kate, he thought, no last-minute slipping out of my responsibilities, no last-minute decision that we owe it to ourselves to be happy. No life ever together. I am utterly committed.

In a moment he would be weeping on this man's shoulder, telling him all about Kate, who did not need any props . . . 'What do you think of my intention to take Julia to Paris this weekend? I've a business reason for going but I thought it might cheer her up.'

'Cheer her up? Well . . .' he shrugged, 'Yes, why not? It's important to have memories. We don't know what's ahead for her, or for you. I'll ask Richard to call in and see her before you go. But, remember, when you feel the glass wall I spoke about, it's time to ask for help . . . from me. And remember also it won't be end of the world.'

'I'll try.'

Leo got up. 'Come and have tea.' He put his arm round Lawrence's shoulders as they walked to the door. 'What a complex being man is,' he said.

Her beauty struck him afresh when they all had tea together. It was as if some burden had been taken off her shoulders, perhaps it was as simple as being given permission to be ill. She seemed to like Aline, who was the typical, logical woman that France often produces, no *nervosité*, no running of her household as if it were a chore as so many Englishwomen seemed to do nowadays. One felt that the benefits were great for Leo and their children.

In the car going back to London she slept a little, again there was the slight almost weightless pressure on his shoulder. When she wakened with the lights of London she said, 'I had such a nice dream, Lawrence. You and I. We were sailing like seagulls high above the world. Nothing troubled us. We had no need to swoop down. We sailed through the blueness and our wings were white and strong. We sailed on for ever . . .'

He remembered that he had forgotten to mention the boy, Crawford North, to Leo. Significant? Not worth mentioning? He was another mystery and there were enough mysteries. Better to get on with solving what lay nearest to hand.

16

He had a strange feeling that it was the end of one life and the beginning of a new one. It was almost like dying. Decisions left you feeling weightless. He didn't feel unduly sad but he had the strong feeling that he wanted his affairs cleared up before they went to Paris. When they came back they would start this new life together, a life where at least in knowing the worst he could hope for a little better.

He wanted to see Kate. To tell her. He didn't know quite what he wanted to tell her, except that he wanted to say what was in his heart. And yet, was that wise? To tell her that he had made a mistake in his life so goodbye? He recognised it as a piece of self-indulgence but he still wanted to see her. Once.

He and Julia had walked through the Kensington streets in the afternoon, and then they had come home and toasted crumpets in front of the electric fire. She was quiet and withdrawn, and she didn't seem to want to go upstairs to work. It was as if she felt the same as he, a sense of imminent change. He asked her once if she had liked Leo and she said yes, he seemed very nice. It was an odd word to use about him. 'You feel happier for seeing him?' he persisted.

'I don't know. I didn't think I was ill.' And then she flared up, 'Why do you all think I'm ill?'

'Just a little, darling. Enough for those who love you to think you should be made well again.'

She said a strange thing, sitting in front of the electric fire, the toasting fork in her hand, 'If this is being ill, I like it. Where would all my strange thoughts go if they make me well? I can wander inside my head, it's like unexplored country.' The landscape of the mind, he thought. The phrase came back to him.

Later he was in the bedroom, packing. They were going off to Paris in the morning. 'But, of course, you'll wear your fur coat?' he asked, and she looked startled. 'No, it's fox fur, I can't take that. Not now . . .'

He told himself that he was getting used to her mysterious reactions, and if he wasn't it was time he did. Leo had warned him. Random changes of thought, he had said, a failure of communication, a feeling that *you* were to blame, that what was being thought or said *ought* to make sense, but didn't.

The doorbell rang and he called, 'I'll get it,' moving swiftly to the door. He wanted to take the first impact of whatever or whoever it was. When he opened it Raymond Mills and his friend stood there. Raymond wore his usual smile, placatory, anxious.

'I'm most awfully sorry, Mr Paton, to intrude. We thought you weren't in at this time, and I said to Roger, it's his half-day, that poor girl needs cheering up. I said, didn't I, Roger, that I was struck by how pale and thin she was getting, absolutely struck. And then I remembered that the last time I was speaking to her she had been most awfully kind and had asked us both in for a cup of coffee and to see her heads.' He didn't know when to stop talking.

'Come in,' Lawrence said, 'she'll be pleased to see you.' He led them into the sitting-room. Julia came out of the bedroom. Had she been hiding? But she was smiling now, obviously glad to see their visitors.

'Hello, dear,' Raymond said, 'Are you feeling better?'

'I'm quite well,' she said abruptly, and then, perhaps seeing Raymond's face, 'it's very kind of you to come in. And you too, Roger.'

'It was Raymond's idea. We was just . . .' he looked at Lawrence as if he wasn't quite sure of his welcome.

'Sit down, won't you?' Lawrence waved. 'I'm afraid the place is a little untidy.'

174

They both sat down on the settee together. Raymond was spokesman again, 'It was just that you said, dear, remember, that we could come in and see your heads and have a cuppa, and I said to Roger, well, that Mr. Paton has been been very generous giving us extra for the ceiling. We bought ever such a nice chicken, and, what else, Roger? Oh, yes, a chocolate mousse from Harrods. Have you ever tried them?'

'Don't forget my shirt,' Roger said.

'That's right,' he flipped his hand in thanks, 'we got Roger a white flowered shirt, white voile with the flowers embroidered in cotton, you know the style?'

'See-through,' Roger said, 'just like yours.'

How do they know that? Lawrence thought.

'So we're ready for the tour round the gallery, dear,' Raymond said.

'I'm not doing any work at the moment. Nothing at all.' Julia stared at the floor and there was a pause.

'Let me offer you a drink,' Lawrence said, knowing that it was too early. 'Gin? whisky?'

'No, really,' Raymond said, 'we never touch spirits.'

'A sherry? Port? I've got some white port.' He found himself insisting vigorously.

'I'd like to try that.' Raymond would please him, of course.

'Roger?' He didn't know his other name.

'I'll take the same, it makes it easier.' He was looking broody, and he suddenly burst out, 'Tell you what, Julia, would you like me to do your hair? Not wash it or anything but put it in rollers then give you a comb out? I do a very good comb out.'

Julia looked at Lawrence. 'You'll be bored,' she said. Her eyes were pleading, he wished fiercely for a moment that she wouldn't look like this, it made him feel like a tyrant, and he wasn't that. He shook his head, smiling.

'Why should I be bored?' And then the idea struck him. 'I tell you what, there's something I want to get from the office since we're going to Paris tomorrow.' It wasn't true.

'Paris, dear! Oh you lucky thing!' Raymond said.

Roger had taken a comb from his breast pocket and was runnning it through his own hair as a preliminary canter. 'Well, you need your hair done for Paris, Julia.'

'Yes, why don't you let Roger do you up? I'm sure he's a wizard with rollers.'

'All right.' She smiled at him. 'You won't be long?'

'No time at all. So, if you'll excuse me,' he handed round drinks, 'I'll get along while you're here. More drinks in the cupboard and coffee in the kitchen. I've just perked some.'

'Don't hurry,' Raymond said, 'we'll keep her company. We'll look after her for you.' His eyes when they met Lawrence's were wise. He felt humbled.

Running downstairs he prayed that Kate would be in. In a way she was the office. Well, that was stretching it a bit. 'A grey lie,' he muttered as he ran to where his car was parked.

She was deeply upset, and yet at peace. She had done the right thing. You always knew when you felt really bad that you had done the right thing. Richard had stayed a long time, saying that the patients would be dying off right, left and centre while he was here. To begin with he had told her that Julia had been to see Leo Susskind, and that he would have the overall care of her. 'I'm glad in many ways,' he had said, 'I'll only be the dogsbody. It's a tricky situation.' She didn't ask questions.

'He thinks that Lawrence is going to be a lot of help to him. In cases like this the relative is just as important as the patient.'

'I'm not prying, Richard, but is there hope that she'll be all right?'

'Leo doesn't forecast. He lives in the present and tries to get the patient to do the same.'

'She's lucky to have him . . .'

'Leo?'

'No, Lawrence.'

He looked at her for a long time, and then he said, 'I'm going to be late for the surgery but now I'm going to talk about us.' This time she listened . . .

So now he was seeing his patient patients and she was sitting quietly on her own. She felt odd, strange, denuded in some way. To think that Richard of all people had dusted off her prejudices, her prudishness and her pride. He had shown himself in a new light, a favourable one. If she could only clear her mind of Lawrence, give him up, give him *up* . . . The doorbell rang and she went quickly, smoothing her dress, making her face glad and welcoming. He must have forgotten something. It was Lawrence.

'Lawrence,' she said, 'what are you doing here?'

'What a gracious welcome!' His smile was forced, 'Were you expecting someone else?'

'In a way. Come in, anyhow.'

'Thank you *so* much.' He pulled a face at her. 'For the purpose of this visit you're the office.'

'Have you left Julia alone?'

'No, she's got two boyfriends there. One of them is setting her hair in what are called giant rollers, and the other one will chatter and keep her amused. No place for a husky male.'

They were in her sitting-room and she saw that the jaunty manner was covering his nervousness. He was pale. 'Sit down. Would you like a drink?'

'No thanks. Kate, forgive this barging in. I had to see you. I've had a traumatic day or two.'

'You went to Dorchester? Richard told me. Did everything go all right?'

'It went.' He got up out of his chair, walked to the window, turned and smiled at her. 'Well, I didn't come

177

here to beat my breast, have no fear.' He laughed, but his eyes were full and moist. 'I don't know *why* I came.'

'Are you turning over a new leaf, perhaps?'

'You're acute. Turning over a new life, rather. Saying goodbye to wishful thinking.'

'Oh . . .' her eyes stung, and she tried to speak lightly, 'I hope you hadn't a dramatic farewell scene in mind.'

'No, dramatic scenes are out.'

'Because we'll bump into each other every day of the week.'

'I know . . .' Don't look at me like that, Lawrence, please don't look at me like that . . .

'She needs me, Kate, God help me, she needs me. Sometimes she puts out a hand to be held. Such sad eyes, Kate, they would wring your heart. I don't know whether there is no hope or a lot of hope. Doctors never really tell you what you want to hear . . . God,' he said, 'I want to sleep with you, God, how I want . . .'

'Shut up,' she said, roughly. 'Have a drink.'

'No, thanks. This is my non-drinking day. Though, let me tell you, I'm no bloody saint.'

'Who is?' She poured herself a strong gin. If he didn't need a drink, she did.

'I'm sick at the thought of what might have been. Let me grizzle for a minute or two, don't listen . . . I've thought about this till I'm blue in the face, but in the end I come back to the fact that she needs me. You're strong, Kate, you don't need me.'

You're wrong, you know. I need you, day and night I need you, I'm about to do a terrible thing, marry one man while loving another.

'Kate, why don't you answer?'

She raised her eyebrows, sipped her gin. 'It's better not to.' It was better not to speak if you thought your mouth would tremble, if you thought that you might throw yourself at this unhappy man with some terrible cliché like, 'Take me, I am thine . . .' Better by far to look enigmatic.

'This psychiatrist, he talked about the glass wall between you and the sick person, between the sick person and reality. I've almost scrabbled against that wall with my fingers, almost but not quite. One has to be prepared for it all the same . . . But, Kate, the poor souls didn't erect it. They didn't ask for it to be erected. Through no fault of their own, perhaps because of heredity, environmental factors, God only knows, the glass wall exists. It might just have been measles, something uncomplicated, and then they would have been better in no time. But with this illness there will be incidents and remissions, elation and depression, the feeling that nothing matters, that they contribute nothing, an existential vacuum he called it. Well, you've got to feel sorry, haven't you? You don't have to be large-hearted to feel sorry, just human . . . They didn't break into a bank, chop up Grandma, Julia, she's so gentle, so gay, so beautiful, she wouldn't wish this sort of thing on herself in a thousand years. If the only contact she has with the outside world at times is my hand, well . . .'

'You've made your point. I believe every word of it. But you shouldn't have come.'

'I know that. Kate . . .' She turned her head away from him, quick springing tears in her eyes, hardly heard him saying, 'But she's pitiable, isn't she? In the end she wins because she is pitiable.'

'Yes, she would win.' She spoke with her head still turned away, her hand to her mouth, 'I couldn't ever do with Julia in bed between us, and just for your ears alone,' she tried to laugh, 'there was a time when I would have done anything to leap into bed with you. Ah, me! But I've got one golden rule. I marry the man I leap into bed with. Isn't that strange for a strong character like me? But you should look behind the labels sometimes, see the shrinking violets masquerading as strong characters. I worked it out long ago. Love isn't as important as being needed, or needing to be needed. And as for my golden rule, the one about leaping into bed, Richard qualifies for my hand, if I may be lady-like. I think in time I may be able to ask you and Julia to come and see us for little dinner parties, I may even yawn when you go . . .'

'Perhaps she won't be at home.' His voice was bleak.

'Hi! I thought you were the non-despairing one.'

'I am. But sometimes I've got a yen to be patted on the head. Do you want a family, Kate?'

'Strange that you should say that. That's one of my chief reasons for getting married. For the last year or so I've had a shameful biological urge, almost got to whipping them out of their prams at supermarkets.'

'Interesting.' He left the window, came towards her.

'Don't kiss me. Don't touch me.' Panic was in her voice. What's that bit about accepting pain, using it, well, here I go. 'And you'd better go too. Have a good time in Paris, and when you see me at the office on Monday morning just give me a gay wave and the top of the morning . . . I feel terrible . . .'

'It's so tragic that I want to laugh.' They were looking at each other now. His smile was lop-sided.

'Will you get to hell out of here? You don't want to see me melt like a lemon jelly, do you? I'm not a good crier, my nose gets red and my face swells.'

She walked to the door with him, opened it. 'My love to Julia.' She reached up and kissed him on the cheek.

She shut the door on him, went back to the room, looked round with her face twisted, went out of it again and into the bathroom where she found what she was looking for, a box of tissues. She went into the bedroom and lay down on the bed, thinking, the luxury of it, let it come . . . but there were no tears. She lay dry-eyed in the dark, even dozing a little, thinking that if someone pricked her with a pin she would feel nothing . . . The doorbell rang again. She went slowly to the door and opened it.

Richard stood there with a bottle in his hand.

'I raced through Surgery,' he said, 'I thought we should celebrate.'

'Aren't you being premature? I might run out on you, yet.'

'No you won't. I know your type. Picture of moral rectitude under all your sophisticated veneer.'

'I thought there had been one lapse, but since you've spotted the priggishness you may come in, but for God's sake will you stop shadowing me?'

'I'm not shadowing you. I just came back in case you were miserable and having second thoughts and needed any help.'

'I don't, and I'm not miserable. Lawrence has been.'

'He's leaving her. Running away with you.'

'Wrong. We, or he, talked about need. Julia needs him, God how she needs him. And you need me to need help. From you. And I need you to need me to need help. Isn't it cosy?' She laughed. 'I tell you what, Richard, let's drink to us. I think we're two very nice people. I'll bring glasses.'

'Champagne glasses.' He waved the bottle proudly.

'You clever thing. Now you've really won me for your own.'

When she came back he took her in his arms because the tears were choking her.

17

So there was the Paris trip and the poignancy that it might be the last trip, but telling himself that he was playing it up like mad, a real Larry Olivier, life was not like that, a series of dramtic incidents. Most of the time nothing much happened, or you thought that nothing much happened, except that when you looked back you saw that this little bit had altered, and then that little bit, and so, gradually, surreptitiously, almost, you found yourself with a totally different situation than what had pertained a year before.

Life cons you, he thought. It leads you on blindfolded, step by step, so that you can rarely have a complete showdown and say, 'That's IT, I've had enough, I quit.' Life does not lack a meaning until the last breath, they told you, the carrot for the donkey.

And on the face of it, this trip was the best trip they had ever had. The plane flight was wonderful with Julia leaning against his shoulder and saying, looking down on the clouds, 'But it's like detergent!' and yes, she would like a cheap gin. And there were the admiring gazes of any man within reach and the turned-down mouth of the air hostess who was used to queening it, the toast of the aircraft.

She loved the lunch on the plastic tray, ate with relish her quiche, her ham with asparagus, her pineapple and cream. She loved the plastic bottle of *eau naturel* and asked the steward if she could keep it. 'I daren't ask for the plastic knives and forks,' she whispered, 'but I'd love them too.' Lawrence remembered as a boy having tea in some café with his mother and begging to be allowed to take home the miniature jar of jam. But you were five, then, he told himself.

And then they drove from Orly into the sunset like a John Wayne film, and the hotel was great because for some reason they had put a sumptuous bouquet of flowers on a pedestal table in the bedroom. 'Lawrence,' she said, 'you arranged it.'

'I did not,' he said, 'I wouldn't know how to arrange for flowers to be in our bedroom in Paris. I'm sure I should have to go via Monsieur d'Estaing, or something.'

'Well, I absolutely adore them and they've done them up even better than I could have done myself.'

So they decided to have that night on the French tiles and tomorrow he would see Parmentier, get the contract signed and possibly give him a mild ticking off for having erratic girlfriends, while Julia looked at the shops.

When she was dressed ready to go out in a Victorian patterned voile dress and a black maxi coat which made her face look incandescent against it, and her hair like . . . 'For God's sake,' he said, kissing her. 'Is there ony other description than spun gold for this stuff?' He lifted a strand in his teeth.

It's all been a bad dream, he thought, as they went down in the lift. This is a highly-strung girl, a good old-fashioned word. Between them, Richard and Leo, aided and abetted by me, have cooked up a situation where none exists. She's still growing up. One of these days she'll say, 'I want a child, Lawrence,' and she'll be a woman, just like that. I'm sorry I made such a fuss, I'm sorry that I ran round whining to Kate . . . Kate, he said, in the midst of his relief about Julia, it's you I love. I've made a great mistake, the mistake of my life. Let Richard be right for you, let Julia become right for me, right for herself, bless us all . . .

They took the Métro to Villiers and went up in the funiculaire to Sacré Cœur. It was pure rubber-necking, of course, and it was fashionable to decry the church, but it had a certain dignity at night with Paris glittering at its feet. And the few people kneeling in prayer, eight, he counted them, well, you couldn't decry them, only envy them.

They walked down the steps to the Place du Tertre and she dismissed it utterly. Her eyes on the paintings were cold. He was amused. Her silent criticism was worse than any comment. Her face was shut and tight as if something had been done to her personally, a psychological rape. He had to take her into a gingham-checked bar for a drink before she relaxed.

On the way back in the Métro a young negro sat

183

with a little girl on his knee not more than two years old, but dressed in a ridiculously grown-up, though miniscule, plastic coat. She turned her cheek against her father's shoulder and slept, and the short upper lip gave the child's face a look of Julia, infinitely tender, touching. The negro's face above the paler-skinned child's was noble in its parenthood, an ancient acceptance, but when Lawrence looked at Julia she was staring into the darkness through the window. When they got back to the hotel they went to bed, and strangely enough they had quiet love and he said this is different and she laughed and said French style. Logical. The mistress gets the trimmings here.

In the morning they went on a *bateau mouche* and that reminded him of Kate, of her quick dark head, of her intelligent comments, 'What are those hooks for on the outside of the houses? Oh, I know, they'll hoist up their furniture that way, the staircases must be too narrow.' He remembered the thick Rembrandt darkness, the feeling of deep happiness, not febrile happiness tinged with fear . . .

But this was rather special too, the pale grey buildings with the flat Renaissance fronts, the thirty-three bridges, the charmed Isle of St. Louis, the Lotus Land, where there were no cinemas or theatres. It was something rather special, nevertheless, to sit and see the whole of Paris sliding past you like a cinema.

He gave her a wad of francs and said she was to have a shopper's lunch in Au Printemps and then buy some presents, but she must consult her map and not stray too far from the parts which she knew. He had to dash off to the Colisée to meet Parmentier. They would meet in the hotel about five o'clock.

Lawrence had said don't get lost, but he had forgotten she knew Paris, and that because of Vevey her French was good. But still, to please him, she would ask directions from this policeman. She was glad he was coloured, they were more civil.

'Excuse me asking also,' she said in rapid French, 'that gentleman who has this moment gone through the gates in his large car, and whom you saluted, he is important?'

'Mademoiselle,' his white teeth flashed, 'you are lucky, you have just seen the General of the French Army.'

'*Vive la France,*' she said.

She loved the Champs Elysée with the tricolours flying, pure Monet, she loved the climatic ambience, the clarity of the atmosphere, the feeling of being twice as much alive here as anywhere else, the feeling that the air was fresh and unused. She bought some *foulards* expensively inscribed, and a tie for Lawrence from Thiéry, and went to the Jeu de Paume. But she came out again feeling depressed. The great set pieces weren't for her, *toujours* Monet, the only one she had lingered at was a little Boudin seascape.

And the sky had clouded and it was raining. Now the speed of the traffic in the Place de la Concorde frightened her where before she had been excited. She stood shivering at the kerb waiting to cross, felt the cruel Spring rain dig into her bones with spiky fingers.

I'm lost, but my feet know Paris . . . They will lead me back to the hotel . . . she followed sheep-like behind a group of people, started to walk towards the Madeleine. I shall remember Paris, I shall remember Lawrence's love. Sometimes I see quite clearly, I have wisdom. There is only for me a long, long tunnel, and at the end, darkness . . . She walked, walked. The sky was grey, it seemed to rest on her shoulders. People scurrying, bright dots, *pointillisme*, since this was Paris.

There are times when I don't want Lawrence, when I don't want anyone, when I wish to be left in my own world, a void, a heavy dark void, but enveloping and somehow comforting . . . when I disintegrate, when there is no longer me, when I become part of the whirlpool . . .

She stopped in front of a boutique, saw the over-worked Parisian elegance, now one would say an old-fashioned elegance, lacking the swinging jauntiness of London, but which was perhaps longer lasting than the frenetic, slightly tatty smartness of London.

She saw her reflection in the window and she stretched out her hand towards it. This is how I stretch out my hand to Lawrence. Help me . . . He doesn't know that each time he saves me from death, not the dying death, but another, far worse, a disintegration . . . she walked on. The rain was steady now, steel grey, like the buildings, people were sheltering in doorways, she saw the white French faces, one zoomed towards her as if seen through a telescope lens, she saw the incipient moustache on the girl's lip.

He doesn't know, she thought, walking on, that I know he loves Kate. *'Pardon, monsieur.'* Black beads for eyes, the appraising French look, logical-sexual . . . That she loves him . . . I've walked too far, I must get to the hotel, feet, take me, padding through the crowds, running a little, so many faces, so many eyes, faces, eyes, faces eyes, *'Pardon, madame,'* it must be near, here is the *Service Libre*, the lingerie shop, the Italian restaurant run by an Egyptian staffed by black-shirted boys, nice boys, ah, here is the hotel, clever feet, and there's the porter who likes me, who rushes forward with my key

'Merci infinement.'

'Vous avez fait une bonne promenade, madame?'

'Oui, merci.' Le clef. Ascenseur. Little gilded cage, *'Aprez vous,'* walk in, mirror with another Julia in it, soaked, her hair black with wetness against her coat, white, white face . . .

'Quel dommage qu'il pleuve.'

'De rien.'

'Troisième étage?'

'Oui, c'est ça. Troisième étage.'

Lawrence folded the contract and put it in its envelope. 'That's your copy, Monsieur Parmentier. I'm glad the business is settled now, I hope you'll be pleased with Monsieur Susskind's translation.'

The man flushed. It would be better now to bring the thing into the open.

'He doesn't bear your friend any grudge for the little contretemps.' What an umbrella of a word! He tried a Gallic shrug. 'Paris! Perhaps you'll make a story out of the incident? Who knows?'

'In my life there are many stories. Some of them are too sad to tell. They would run with blood. I'm grateful to Monsieur Susskind for his kindness and forbearance.'

Lawrence didn't speak. The affair seemed to be finished in more ways than one. 'And now, if you'll excuse me, I must get back. I'm dining out with my wife and going to the theatre.'

'Quite so. I'm sorry you couldn't have been my guest. I thank you for the luncheon.'

'Some other time.'

'I hope so.' They both rose. He thought that Parmentier had a sheep-like face, but the adjective only applied to its length, a Fernandel face, the long rounded chin, the lugubrious air. The eyes were full and dark, tired but intelligent. Lawrence hoped there would be many books from him. He was sufficiently *avant-garde* for the Englishman's conception of a French author, coming nicely between Simenon and Sagan, with perhaps a dash of Robbe-Grillet for style. They liked their *nouvelle vague* not to be too vague.

When he reached the hotel and had taken the lift to their bedroom, he found Julia sitting up in bed. Her cheeks were flushed. She looked guilty.

'What's wrong, darling?' he asked, sitting down beside her, 'Why are you in bed?' He recognised the gnawing unease in himself, moved in his seat as if to shake it off, smiled to hide it.

'I think I got a chill. Don't be cross. I walked too far in the rain and I was shivering.'

He took her hands. He could feel her pulse leaping under his fingers. 'We ought to get a doctor.'

'No, we mustn't, it's a trifle of a cold, a travel cold, it was just that I thought I should be warmer in bed. But I'm getting up now. We've got to have that last dinner in Paris.'

'Do you feel like eating?'

She was jolly, almost rumbustious, her eyes denied it. 'Do I feel like eating! Remember I'm a Cordon Bleu. I'm in my spiritual home. This is going to be a meal that I'll remember, that I'll remember . . . help me to get up.'

'You sound like the Lady of the Camellias.' He spoke lightly to hide his worry.

'Well, I don't feel like her. I'm bursting with good health. Paris always does this to me. Look, I'm ready to go except for my dress.' She swept back the bedclothes and he saw her thin body clothed in a short satin slip, her long legs in tights, the thin ankles.

'You've got an Afro hair-cut.' She must have been towelling her hair and it spun and danced round her face, round the hectic pink of her cheeks, the dark blue of her eyes. The skin around them was egg-shell white, delicate. I shall never see her more beautiful, he thought. What a wife she would have made if only . . . cut it out, he thought, cut it out . . .

He put his arms under her and she clung round his neck. Her body was hot against his. 'Are you sure you feel well enough?'

'Yes, I'm all right. It's important to go . . . it's important to me . . .'

'You win.' He kissed her swiftly in case she would notice the unease which now seemed chronic.

She picked at her food, but she charmed the waiter who stood on his head to please her, brought special dishes, special sauces, putting the whole kitchen at her command. She laughed with him but her eyes had a heavy sadness when she looked across the table at Lawrence, and a kind of wisdom, nothing to do with worldliness, but rather the clear uncluttered wisdom of a child. A ridiculous notion came to him, that she was saying goodbye, but he thought, what nonsense. She was in his care and protection for evermore, wasn't she, his special privilege on this earth to love and cherish.

They went to the theatre, a show about youth, and its sweet stridency assaulted his senses, making him feel old and tired. It was too long ago since he was young, there was no message here for him. Julia was unmoved, except once on a little plateau of silence a French boy sang into the microphone, huskily poignant, and there was a silence in the audience too. Only the French voice adapted itself to this kind of song, French images rose in the mind, the streets, the cafés, the sadness of love, *l'amour*.

When they came back to the hotel the attentive porter hurried forward. Had they had a good evening? You went to . . .? '*Ah, vous avez beaucoup de courage!*' Yes, he had seen the show as well, he had even danced on the stage with the company. His wife had pushed him, but, yes, in the end he had gone, Oo-la-la!

Julia was vibrant now, her cheeks flushed, he knew men in the lounge were drawn to look at her, she created an island of beauty amongst the fake Louis Fourteenth fauteuils. He should be used to it by this time. Her French, which was always more than adequate, broke away from her in verbal rushes punctuated by laughter, the porter was in the seventh heaven of delight, what a story to tell Fifi when he got home, this beauty in the hotel . . . the rapport was strong. Lawrence felt stultified, too literal, and out in the cold.

The next morning she seemed better, and there was the incandescent look he had first seen at Wimbledon, the inner glow, the radiance. But her eyes were glittering strangely, a hard glitter obscuring the gentleness, and her cheeks were still their unusual pink. She sat silently beside him in the plane, and when he held her hand it was burning hot. 'We'll get you home, darling.' Once he brushed her hot cheek with his lips. When she turned to him, her eyes were as they had been in the restaurant, weighted with sadness, the glitter gone. A prisoner's eyes.

His heart was sore, a physical soreness. 'We'll get you home . . .' He remembered that Richard had told him that toxicity might bring on an attack, and he was miserable because he thought, nothing is ever clear-cut, one longs to have it clear-cut, but that's life. Here we are again, the same doubts, the same indecision. If she becomes strange and ill I shan't know if it is because she's fevered, because she's caught a feverish cold . . . For a moment he was full of self-pity.

But when he had paid the taxi, and had run beside her up the stairs because it was hard to keep up with her as if she was seeking the sanctuary of the flat, he began to think that there wasn't so much doubt. And he was afraid. And when he looked at her strange face as she went rushing into the sitting-room, he thought, this is not my Julia . . .

'What are you looking for, darling?' he asked. He heard his voice shaking.

'Nothing . . . nothing . . .' Her face was absorbed, he was nothing too, he wasn't there, she turned over some magazines on the table, stopped, looked down at them, or her hands, because she stopped leafing the pages then went quickly out of the room.

Standing where he was, and listening, at first it was like a running conversation between two people, but there was only Julia. And when he went into the bedroom, and found her sitting on the bed, she looked at him and she didn't know him, she didn't know him . . . Her eyes were huge, dark, empty, the whites clear round the pupil, they looked through him. And there was a half-smile on her face. She picked at the candlewick bedspread with nervous fingers as the steady stream of words broke from her lips...

'Paris city of love. Why don't you wear your fox fur, Julia? The fox was running, running, the footsteps were of blood but Lawrence took care of me Roger did my hair . . .' She put one hand up, felt her hair, got up and looked into the mirror for a long time. The words were inaudible at first, then they came in a full rush like a turned-on tap.

'For your husband he said, to make you nice for you husband . . . Raymond I'm sorry about the ceiling did you have your umbrella up because it would stop the water . . . Kate did it . . . Kate . . . Kate . . . She took him away but she was kind the cat she was kind the cat is still there if you tiptoe you can hear it . . .' She wheeled round, still with her stranger's eyes, her eyes of black glass. Her finger was to her lips, 'Tiptoe you hear it but I'll go upstairs and see the children. I don't like the children now Sue is spoiled . . .' Her face crumpled, she hid it in her hands but when she raised it she was smiling . . . 'When I get home I'll see Leo and say, Leo, what will I say, is there some pill, there must be some pill . . .'

He couldn't stand it. He turned and walked into the sitting-room, felt the tears thick in his eyes. For God's sake, he stuck his fists in them, went over to the telephone, turned his back to the door because the tears were now coursing down his cheeks, and really, since they were coming so thick and fast who cared about wiping them for God's sake?

He flipped open the pad to find Richard's number, he heard her voice, louder now, she must be standing at the door. 'I can smell the cat. No it wasn't her room it was the room in the hotel in Paris where Crawford made love to her. Crawford why is your back to me? It was Leo, he wasn't kind, he would take her away, she would walk faster about the room he wouldn't find her . . .' he heard

191

her rapid footsteps . . . 'faster faster faster pull on the brakes mind that black patch, the poor tree the poor fox, now she could see it was Lawrence, dear Lawrence, not Crawford. He would take her to the soft moony universe, Beulah, Beulah, what a pretty name Cuckoo Wood I'll wear my fox fur coat when I go run harder it's behind you black fur fox fur black hissing hide in the ditch, safe here, see the little bird no not safe not safe at all he's there growing bigger blacker blotting out the sun . . .' It wasn't her voice, it was a child's, thin, a child's terrified voice.

'Richard,' he said, 'could you come at once. And will you phone Leo.'

He listened to Richard's professional advice, he felt years older than he, he was calm and cool. There was a feeling of elation almost, a satisfaction that he at last knew where he stood, that he was stretched. Everyone welcomed a challenge, everyone liked facing up to the enemy, if they knew what it was, in the end. When you go down far enough you can only come up. There was a strange happiness to be found in a situation which could only get better.

She was pulling at his sleeve, talking, talking, and he turned to pinion her in his arms, gently, because she was his wife.